Right Out of a Movie

She viewed the killers' approach with inner calm. The heroine got away at the end, she remembered. So Ronnie looked at their blank, shiny faces without worry. She ignored their blood-caked weapons. In her addled brain, she felt certain that they could not harm her. She was the one who survived.

Her twisted thinking was confirmed for a split second when she heard the voice coming from behind the leather mask. Then there was nothing between her and instant insanity.

"You got away in the movie," the man in the leather mask told her. "But we're changing the ending." Then they fell upon her.

Books by Wade Barker

Published by
WARNER BOOKS

NINJA MASTER

#6
DEATH'S DOOR

Wade Barker

WARNER BOOKS

A Warner Communications Company

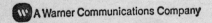

NINJA MASTER

#6
DEATH'S DOOR

Chapter One

The movie had been terrible.

It was one of those screaming slash-'em-ups Todd enjoyed so much. If he had his way that's all the four of them would ever see: horrible, sadistic films where young people were murdered in almost every conceivable manner. Ronnie glanced at Todd's profile from across the front seat of the car. By all outward appearances he was the blond, bland, good-looking, well-built young man Ronnie's parents saw. But they didn't see him like this, away from their large suburban California house, happily babbling away to Brian in the back seat about the "neat" film deaths.

"And do you remember the scene where the scarf got caught in the cycle's gears and pulled his face into the spinning spokes?" he called out, his words resounding off the Mustang's windshield. "Pretty good special effects, huh?"

"Yeah," Brian agreed, leaning forward. "I'd like to know how they did that thing with his nose. They must've had thin hoses under some fake skin to pump out all the blood, but I still can't figure out how they ripped that hunk out of his nose."

"It must've been a fake face," Todd replied, really into the bloodthirsty spirit of the effect. "They must've made

7

a cast of the actor's face, then filled the fake head with guts and stuff. It was all fake."

"Well, I think it was all disgusting!" Becky interrupted, rising from her huddled position in the backseat next to Brian. "How can you two talk that way? Why do we always go to see these things?"

"Well, gee," Todd said with feigned innocence, glancing into the rear with a grin. "I thought you liked these movies, Beck."

"I hate them and you know it, Ingram," the brunette in the back seat replied, using Todd's surname. "The only reason I go is that you three always outvote me."

"Now, don't drag me into this." Ronnie spoke up for the first time during the trip home. "The only reason I go is that Todd would drag me by the hair if I said I wouldn't. Remember, if it wasn't for me, we wouldn't have seen 'Ordinary People' or 'The Elephant Man.'"

"Yeah," Brian said with exaggerated relish. "I'd like to know how they did the nose in that one too." Becky slapped him on the arm for that crack. He fell back into the seat, his arms raised in supplication.

"But those were on videotape," Becky complained. "And we saw them at your house. The only time we ever go out to the movies is to see these knife things. Why don't you guys watch those on tape and leave us out of it?"

"Aw, it's no fun that way," Todd complained. "Go on, Beck, admit it. You love going to the movies."

"Yeah, I like to go," Becky replied with a pout. "But not to these things. Everybody's smoking, and yelling, and throwing things. I can't take it any more." She slumped back into her seat, pulling her legs under her. The conversation stalled as she looked out the window at the passing night lights along the highway.

Ronnie took the moment to check her face in her pocketbook mirror. She knew why Todd and Brian liked going to see these murder movies. Even if the film wasn't scary, she and Becky had little choice but to cling to their dates in either disgust or fear. If what was happening on-screen didn't get to them, the environment would. These movies were like roller coaster rides: predictable, frightening, and just a little bit dangerous.

Looking in the mirror, she could understand why Brian and Todd were so eager to squeeze or get squeezed by their dates. The face gazing back at her from the glass was fresh, blond, and beautiful. The eyes were crystal blue and round, the nose was small and pert, the mouth was rich and well-shaped, and the hair was long, flowing, and almost curled, giving her mane a "wet look." She glanced down at her seated figure. Her breasts were nice: not too big or too small and muscular under the T-shirt. Her waist was slim and her legs were long and sleek under the denim of her designer jeans. Even her feet were attractive in her medium-heeled, open-toe sandals.

Ronnie shifted the mirror so she could see the back seat. Becky was still looking out the window. The blond in the front was not so self-centered that she couldn't admire the brunette in the back. Becky's hair was rich and wavy, and her figure was well set off by the jogger's suit she was wearing—running shorts and a red terry cloth V-necked top. But instead of sneakers, she wore ankle-strapped heels. Her legs were not as long as Ronnie's but they were creamy smooth and handsome in the pale blue light coming through the Mustang's windows.

Ronnie clicked her pocketbook shut, looking over at Todd. He was looking back at her with a wistful, slightly embarrassed smile, as if saying, *Becky has a point, but what can you do? When you're slightly warped, you're slightly warped.* But the brunette took the pocketbook closing as a cue to speak up again.

"And you know something, you guys?" she said decisively, turning back from the window. "I'm not going to take it anymore." She slapped the vinyl covering of her seat. "I mean, we've seen everything. I've been to the last house on the left, I know better than to answer the phone, look in the basement or go into the attic. I've celebrated Halloween, Mother's Day, and black Christmas. I've been to prom night and met Carrie. What's left?"

"Thanksgiving?" Brian answered jokingly. He got slapped on the arm again.

"I'm serious," Becky retorted. "That's it. If you guys want to go to these things, you can go without me."

"Aw, come on, Beck...," Todd began.

"I mean it!" Becky exclaimed, a touch of stridency in her voice. "I don't enjoy them and I won't be subjected to them just because you guys are sick!"

Brian was the first to realize just how upset she was. He moved over to put his arms around his girl. Becky resisted at first, but then returned his embrace, frowning. "That's all right," said her brown-haired boyfriend, patting her on the back.

Todd's look of embarrassment turned to consternation. Now he'd have to come face to face with why he wanted to see those movies. Ronnie couldn't help but smile. For all his bravado, Todd secretly feared he was just as yellow as anybody else. He wouldn't go to the knife-kill flicks alone. He would only go in a group so he could show his nerve by laughing at all the sadistic, torturous deaths.

"We've seen some pretty bad movies," Ronnie took up the verbal attack, "but really, Todd, tonight was the worst. Not only was it vicious, but it was boring."

"Yeah," Todd admitted. "Maybe the genre is played out."

"Well, if *it* isn't," Ronnie replied,"*we* are. I think this should be the last one we see."

"For a long, long time," Brian added.

"Forever," Ronnie corrected, looking back at him. He looked up and shrugged. Ronnie turned her attention to her own boyfriend. "Well?"

Todd twisted uncomfortably in the driver's seat. "Okay," he finally agreed. "Okay, okay." He slowed the car and turned the wheel. The Mustang glided off the highway and onto an exit ramp. Becky applauded his decision from the backseat.

"All right!" she proclaimed. "And tomorrow, can we go out and see something good?"

"What?" said Todd. "One of those weird foreign flicks?"

"I'm sure there's something good playing made right here in Hollywood that doesn't have one knife or drop of blood in it," Ronnie patiently reprimanded him.

"Probably got Alan Alda in it," the blond driver muttered. "All right, we'll go see something *good*."

"Promise?" Becky called.

"Cross my heart," Todd answered. "And hope to die."

The Mustang wound through the suburban streets as Becky leaned forward and happily conferred with Ronnie about the romances, dramas, and comedies she wanted to see. They were still deciding when the car left most of the split-levels and one-story ranches behind. The car moved along the quiet, nearly empty private roads that wound along in front of sprawling mansions with large, perfectly manicured lawns. Todd took a left between two stone columns and drifted up the driveway to Ronnie's house.

The blond girl's father had made a fortune from foreign stocks and he had bought a prime piece of U.S. real estate with his profits. Even in house-happy, land-hungry Southern California, the place was at least two hundred fifty yards from the nearest neighbor. It was very quiet and very private. Nothing seemed out of the ordinary to Ronnie as she got out of the car. Her father's Mercedes was in the driveway and her mother's BMW was in the garage. Her own Datsun 280Z was parked beside the Bavarian auto. Since it couldn't seat four, they had taken Todd's Mustang.

The lights were on outside, in the living room, her father's upstairs den, and the master bedroom. Her dad was probably still up working while her mother was watching cable TV, she decided. She felt a sudden chill across her shoulders and her brow furrowed, but she forgot about the strange sensation when Todd put his arm around her. Her subconscious told her that the chill was caused by the air displaced before Todd's approaching arm. The idea that something might be wrong did not occur to her until it was too late.

Later, like it was part of a "what's wrong with this picture" puzzle, she would recall that she was used to seeing her parent's moving silhouettes inside. But on this night, there was no visible movement. All the motion was outside as the two pairs of teenage lovers hopped up the stairs to the front door. Ronnie turned the knob and pushed, revealing a grand front foyer. Almost without thought, the group marched to the right toward the living room.

"We're home!" Ronnie called out diffidently, not really expecting an answer. And she didn't get one.

She had let Brian and Becky enter first, so she and Todd brought up the rear as they left the foyer and walked through the dark dining room toward the living room light. Brian was looking at his girl, Becky was looking back at Ronnie. The blond returned the other girl's gaze. Only Todd looked ahead, and all he saw was part of the long, white couch and the beige drapes closed over the picture window beyond. But he knew from experience that to their immediate left as they entered would be another stairway leading up and, beyond that, a door to the kitchen.

"I know just what we'll do," Becky happily proclaimed. "We'll go to the early show of a really good film, then we'll go out for a really good meal, and then we'll go out dancing. It'll be the first satisfying evening we've had in a long time. Just imagine, no fast food burgers, no pinball, and no blood and guts!"

On that note, the quartet entered the living room. Ronnie saw something out of the corner of her eye. But rather than look in that direction, she looked the other way. Even so, she saw something out of the corner of the other eye as well. Her gaze abruptly returned straight forward. The two brunettes in front of her fell against each other as she felt Todd surge against her side. The next moment she heard the sickeningly wet smack and a rush of air. A second after that she sensed another rush, this time one of shock, and a sensation like many tiny, sharp-legged bugs crawling up her body.

As soon as the teenagers had entered the room, a trio had descended upon them. Someone had dropped on Todd from the stairs, smashing him on the side of the head with a hammer. As the blond boy crumpled with a rasping sigh, the same person wrapped his arms around Ronnie, lifting her right off the plush pale carpet. Another man emerged from against the wall to hit Brian across the temple with a wrench. A third man, the biggest of the three, moved at the same time, grabbing Becky.

She managed a short, frightened scream before the air was crushed out of her and she was thrown stomach first against the third man's shoulder, kicking and swinging her fists. The man who had slugged Brian moved toward Ronnie, the dripping red tool still in his hand. The blond girl's attention was wrenched off the other girl as the second man neared. She suddenly realized that three psychos were attacking them in her own house as a strange and terrifying face loomed up into her vision.

It was a human face, but it was neither Caucasian or Negro. It was literally black and white. The second man had made himself up so that one half of his face was the color of coal and the other was the color of chalk. Above the thick caking was greasy black hair. Ronnie closed her eyes to the visage, arched her back and opened her mouth to scream. The black and white man used his other hand to pull out a patterned red handkerchief the size of a dish towel from his back pocket and started stuffing it into Ronnie's open mouth just as she managed to get some sound out.

Her eyes opened widely as she felt the coarse material which smelled of oil being pressed against her lips. She kicked out and tried to raise her hands toward the gag. But just as she reached up, the arms holding her let go and she dropped to the floor. The combination of her heels and the thick carpet pile threw her off balance. Rather than pulling the cloth out of her mouth, she had to push her arms out for balance. But then the hands that had held her clamped around her wrists and wrenched them up behind her back. A sudden shock of shoulder pain combined with the sensation of choking to send Ronnie's mind into paroxysms of hysteria.

She fell to the carpet, her arms still held tightly behind

her. She ignored the pain across her chest as she tried to force the handkerchief out with her tongue. But just as she got the tip of it placed against the material, a thick rope was wrapped between her teeth, pushing her tongue down and her teeth apart. She felt the rope being pulled taut and then it was wrapped around her head and through her teeth again. She tasted the rope's edge at the corners of her mouth. The only sounds she heard were the heavy breathing of the man behind her, the stifled giggles of the man gagging her, the sharp screeches of Becky, and her own muffled, moist bleatings. She couldn't understand it. Why gag her and let Becky scream for all she was worth? It didn't make sense.

New waves of terror were added to old. She felt a knee at the top of her back, the prickly weight of the rope wrapping around her wrists, and her feet kicking ineffectively against the thick carpet. She strained to raise her head, moving it from side to side, trying to loosen the tight coils which held the oily handkerchief in place. Her eyes closed, she felt a curtain of sweat across her face. Eyes open, she could see through the kitchen door.

She saw the big third man slowly and purposefully carry Becky toward the wrought iron pot and pan hanger on the far wall. She saw that all of the kitchen utensils had been removed from the fixture, revealing its basic design: a metal spiderweb of sharp iron hooks. A horrifying feeling of certainty flooded Ronnie's brain; she suddenly knew exactly what the third man was planning. She tried to scream again, only to hear the noise burble out of her mouth in the form of drool.

But nothing was keeping Becky from screaming. Confused, frustrated, and frightened, she let out a cry every chance she got. She would suck in breath and then push it out again in the form of a high-pitched shriek every few seconds. It did her no good because the only people who could hear it were inside the house. Ronnie felt tears freely flowing out of her eyes. She was looking at Becky, and Becky was looking back at her. As much as the brunette twisted in the big man's grip, she could not see the maze of hooks toward which he was carrying her. Ronnie could.

Ronnie saw the man throw Becky forward and then felt her stomach heave and turn as the brunette slammed against the metal framework. Then, even worse, she saw Becky settle onto many hooks, her weight making them dig in and hold.

The smaller girl stopped screaming. She remained skewered to the wrought iron fixture, her limbs askew and her eyes wide. She was adjusting to an all-encompassing sensation of pain she had never felt before. For a blissful second, her mind was overloaded. She was simply unable to accept what had happened to her. Tragically, the mind is incredibly resilient. It adjusted, but her tolerance for pain vanished. Her screams started anew, only this time with the added message of excruciating anguish.

Ronnie's vision was blurred for a moment with tears and then she was grabbed again and hurled back. Suddenly she was thrown against the wall at the foot of the stairs, back first. Then she slid down to sit with her hands bound behind her. She could no longer see Becky's torture, but saw instead the black-and-white man binding her ankles while another man looked on with a strange vacuous expression. The blond then realized that the other man's expression was blank because he was wearing a false face—a rubber mask that portrayed a wrinkled, hook-nosed, wispy-haired old man.

Ronnie tried to push herself away in shock, but the

16

wall behind her would not give. She strained against the rope that held her arms, but it afforded her no further freedom. Finally, they finished binding her ankles, preventing any movement of her legs at all.

The black-and-white man and the wispy-haired old man straightened and stepped back to survey their handiwork. They saw a beautiful blond girl sweating, writhing, and chomping down on coils of thick, tight hemp. Her shoulders painfully rubbed against the designer wallpaper behind her, making her curved hips slide against the carpet and her breasts jut against her top. Her handicapped, tortured movements were accompanied by the screams coming from the kitchen.

The two attackers looked at each other—the man without the mask wore an expression of delight. Then they looked back at their captive. Ronnie heard words coming from behind the old-man mask.

"Sit tight honey," he said. "We got something to do, but we'll be back real soon." The man in the mask moved away from her first. The black-and-white man remained for a second to add his own suggestion.

"Don't go no place," he advised with a giggle. Then he joined his partner in grabbing the awakening form of Brian. The brown-haired youth was groaning and moving on the floor when the attacking duo gripped him by the shoulders and knees. With casual strength they pulled him up and carried him into the kitchen like a sack of potatoes.

From her position, Ronnie could watch their progress between the stair's bannister uprights. She saw them trot him up to the butcher block table in the middle of the room and throw Brian atop it. The shock of his landing woke Brian up completely. But before he was able to do anything about his ignominious position, his two carriers took hold of his wrists and ankles, pulling him spread-eagled across the thick wood surface. Ronnie saw him pull and twist in their grip, but the lithe young man's strength was obviously no match for his two assailants. They held him in place as if he were a child.

Brian was about to shout in surprise and anger when he noticed the contorting, blood streaked girl above him to the left. He looked over in that direction, speechless. Becky looked to him in total terror and supplication. Her limbs moved feebly as crimson liquid continued to pour out of her gaping wounds and course down her body. Her expression said that she knew she was dying but still hoped for some kind of help from the man she had come to love and depend on.

Brian's horrified gaze went from his girl friend to the hulking figure in front of her. As he looked, the third man turned toward him. He was tall—nearly six feet, eight inches—and fat. His large, soiled yellow shirt hung over his waistband, but there was no disguising the hefty rolls of fat circling his torso. There was also no hiding the musculature of his shoulders and arms. What was disguised was his face. But rather than makeup or a Halloween mask, the third man was wearing different camouflage: a featureless sheet of dark brown leather, with holes for his brown eyes, his small nose, and his thick-lipped mouth.

Brian had only that moment to gaze at his executioner. In the next second, the third man moved forward, nimbly plucking a cleaver from the magnetized holder above the table. Without pausing, the third man gripped Brian's left arm with one hand and buried the steel blade in his shoulder with the other.

Ronnie turned her eyes from the horrendous sight,

feeling bile rise in the back of her throat. By a herculean effort, she kept from throwing up. With the foul cloth in her mouth, she knew she would choke on her own puke. And somehow, for some reason, she was not suicidal. All her energy was concentrated on survival. For no reason she could fathom, she had been hurled into an irrational world of violent death. But her own pride and humanity would not let her give in to it.

As she heard Brian's rending screams of extreme torment register vaguely in the back of her mind, she doubled her efforts to free herself from her bonds. But as much as she twisted her arms, the ropes around her hands would not loosen. They were cunningly tied so that each wrist was bound in its own coil of hemp. They were not simply tied together side by side like her ankles. Ronnie felt blood at her wrists and at the corners of her mouth from the rough strands, but she also felt a greater mobility at her legs. By pulling and kicking, she felt the loops widen.

She was making so much progress in that endeavor that she hazarded a glance in the kitchen's direction to make sure none of the attackers had noticed. It was a mistake. First she saw the still jittering corpse of Brian, almost completely dismembered. His eyes were open and staring back at her as his torso jerked and flopped on the cutting board. The rest of the kitchen looked like a steaming slaughterhouse. Dribbling sheets of blood were everywhere, with guts oozing onto the floor.

But what seemed worse—even worse than the third man chopping at Brian's right leg, his left leg already severed at mid-thigh and his arms tattered stumps—was what the black-and-white man was doing to the brunette girl. He was standing on a chair so he was even with her hanging form. He had already pulled off her shorts and pushed her legs apart. Now he was cutting off her underwear and fumbling with his own belt.

Ronnie looked away, almost driven crazy by the sight. Her own struggle subsided for a moment as she tried to comprehend the vicious insanity of the attackers' actions. She looked the other way, only to see Todd's unconscious form staining the carpet from the wound on his temple. A fleeting mental glimpse of him rising from the floor with two blazing guns in his hands reached her brain before a more realistic vision replaced it.

The blond girl remembered Todd's face illuminated by the flickering images of a movie. These images were of a brunette girl screaming and writhing on a hook as her boyfriend was dismembered. But the faces of the dying were not those of Brian and Becky. They were other faces that Ronnie recalled with a frightening feeling of déjà vu. She had witnessed this scene before.

That realization sent the girl back to renew her struggle. With sudden strength, she slid off her shoes and pulled her legs out from their circular, cuffed prison. Quickly and with a muscle-twisting effort, she got her legs beneath her, pushed her feet flat against the floor and stood up. Flat against the wall, her view of the kitchen was blissfully blocked. With a last look at Todd, Ronnie crept away from the living room.

Quietly, without even realizing that she was holding her breath, the blond entered the darkened dining room. She stopped just long enough to take a look at the swinging door that connected it with the kitchen. All she saw was the line of illumination around the top, bottom, and side. But in that illumination, she could pick out the unmistakable trail of blood bubbling onto the polished wood floor from the other side. For some strange reason she thought of the scene in "The Shining" where blood poured out of an elevator door.

Another pang of dèjá vu assailed her, a feeling she rejected immediately. Instead, she pushed herself forward toward the brightly lit foyer, the front door, and, with any luck, freedom beyond.

But her luck had run out. Just as she was about to hobble out into the front room, a figure disengaged himself from the shadows of the far dining-room wall. It was the wispy-haired old man. He popped out, blocking her way. She tried to scream as she unavoidably bounced against him, but the sodden cloth in her mouth blocked almost all the sound she could make. She backed away from his figure, then whirled to run back into the living room. The man in the leather mask was blocking her return, the bloody meat cleaver still in his hand.

This "girl in the middle" tableau froze until the third man started moving forward. With a shriek that even her gag couldn't eliminate, the blond spun back toward the foyer and ran. With nimble desperation, she managed to avoid the clawing fingers of the wispy-haired old man. She had to twist and scrape along the front wall, but she got past him and out into the sparkling foyer. Without looking back, she ran to the front door.

Upon her arrival, however, she was forced to look back. She had to turn so that her bound hands could grip the doorknob. As she felt the knob slip in her sweaty palms, she saw that the two attackers had moved to each other's side and were slowly, deliberately moving toward her. The sight of their approaching blank faces, big bodies, and clenching hands was all the motivation Ronnie needed. She spun the door knob, flung it open and hurled herself out the open door.

She fell right into the open arms of the black-and-white man. He grabbed her tightly around the waist, sunk his fingers into her damp hair, pulled her head back, opened his mouth and planted a messy kiss on her gagged lips. She felt his tongue on her teeth before she wrenched herself away, hearing his laughter as she lost her balance and fell. She dropped to her knees inside the house as the black-and-white man closed the door behind her.

"I told you not to go no place," he admonished lightly.

His casual, bright tone both infuriated and scared her. She was trapped and helpless at the hands of three men who saw other people as mere hunks of meat to be abused or slaughtered. She forced herself to think of some kind of survival plan. The only image her mind would serve up to her, however, was that of her strong, capable father. She saw him in his den, smiling against the backdrop of the rough-hewn wooden wall and the hunting rifles he had mounted over the fireplace.

The thought of the guns sent Ronnie back to her feet again. She stood in the center of a triangle the three attackers had made with their upright bodies. She ran in between the old man and the leather mask to the main stairway. She leaped up the steps two at a time, her teeth clamping down on the wet rope in her mouth. She reached the apex of the steps and raced to the right toward her father's study. Behind her she could hear the thudding, measured steps of the three killers.

The stairway threw the title and images of the movie "Psycho" into her brain. And her pursuers' slow, heavy steps recalled scenes from "Night of the Living Dead." Again, the horrid feeling of dèjá vu twinged throughout her being. It was all so familiar somehow. Once again she forced the cinematic images from her thoughts. She navigated the dark hallway from memory until she reached her father's thick door. She turned her back to it so that her raw, bleeding hands could grip its latch. Again she was forced to look back the way she had come. There, at the top of the stairs, lit from the foyer below, were the shadowy silhouettes of the crazed trio. They stood motionless in the dark at the top of the stairs, their hands dripping.

Ronnie got the latch loose, pushed the door open with her back and stumbled into her father's study. Even as she turned toward his desk, she felt sure he was already dead. But even that subconscious warning did not prepare her for the sight of his corpse.

His high-powered hunting rifle—a Remington Model 1100 shotgun—was off the wall. In its place were most of the man's brains. The gun's butt was on the floor, the end of its barrel in his mouth. His lips were wrapped around it like a baby sucking on a milk bottle. His eyes were open but only the whites showed. A thin halo of red-flecked white hair circled a rotting crater where the back and top of his head use to be. The entire scene was lit by the flickering embers in the fireplace.

This vision blasted into Ronnie's consciousness with the power of a howitzer. It drove her back, gasping for breath, against the connecting door to the master bedroom. Desperate to get away, she slammed her shoulder against the partition, then scrambled to get her fingers around the knob. She gripped, twisted, pulled, and then swung inside the next room.

Her mother's death had been blissfully peaceful by comparison. She merely rested—naked—at the foot of the bed in a position of deep entreaty. Knees bent, bowed down, she seemed to be praying. The only things out of the ordinary were the three holes in the back of her head.

Ronnie looked from the corpse to the bedroom door

as she heard it open. The three murderers entered. She backed away, her head shaking, pleading noises coming out of her mouth from behind the gag. Calmly, they circled the bed and continued to approach her without a word. She continued to back up. Soon it became evident that they were shepherding her. She couldn't understand why or to where until she felt the cool glass on her perspiration covered back. She was standing right up against the large French doors that led out to the small balcony overlooking the family greenhouse.

Ronnie was standing in the middle of the left-hand door, far enough away from the door latch so that she couldn't get her fingers around it. Within seconds, all three killers had closed in so that she couldn't move without touching one of them. She looked into their disguised, blank faces and felt her legs go weak. But before she could fall, all three placed their hands on her torso. The big man in the leather mask pushed against her head, neck, and shoulders. The wispy-haired old man was pushing against her ribs and stomach. The black and white man was grinding and pushing his mitts against her breasts.

The pressure was incredible. They seemed to be using all their strength to force her against the glass partition. She couldn't breathe. A yellow-orange haze colored her vision and blanked out their intent faces. Her bound wrists were pressed against her rear end. She tried to kick out but her legs felt like two tubes filled with gravel. Still, she didn't lose consciousness. She felt all the pain and all the pressure. She felt her bones shifting and the doorframe giving way. She was sure that within seconds either her chest would cave in or the door would break open.

Neither happened. Instead, Ronnie suddenly found herself hurtling through the glass, which had shattered around her. She fell among the spinning, glinting shards, her flesh pierced everywhere by the cascade of razor-sharp edges. She fell sideways on a bed of the wicked points and then even more fell on top of her. She could feel sharp cuts in some areas of her body while other parts deadened out completely, like radio outposts suddenly bombed into silence by the enemy.

She groaned and rolled onto her back. The three men were still standing on the other side of the now shattered partition. They saw a once beautiful girl straining against still tight ropes in a pool of broken glass and her own blood. The red liquid was dripping from her wrists, her lips, her nose, her cheek, her side, her chest, her back, one thigh, and all over her feet. Her hair was matted and her eyes teary and bloodshot.

The men examined their handiwork for a moment and then the big man in the leather mask took two steps forward, leaned down, grabbed the girl and threw her over the edge of the balcony as if she were a Raggedy Ann doll.

Ronnie didn't know where she was, but she welcomed the relieving sensation of floating for a brief second. The world whirled around her and then was reflected back to her eyes by the glass roof of the greenhouse. She smashed through it, receiving only the most oblique sensations of sharpness in her mind. Finally the floating stopped. She felt her body come to rest, but it seemed as if her soul went on, drifting from her as if attached to her skin with rubber bands.

But then, horribly, it returned inside of her, making her aware of the incalculable pain and the relentless horror of her situation. She longed to hurl herself on one of the glass shards to end it all, but she could not move. She had all but eaten the oily cloth in her mouth, so she could have screamed around the rope. But try as she might, the only human noises in the night were her tiny pain-ridden gasps.

She did not know how long it was between the time she was thrown and the time the man in the leather mask returned to retrieve her. All she knew was that it was still dark when the hulking figure appeared on the ground and scooped her up like an ape lifting a kitten. She was carried back into the house and dropped onto the living room sofa, her blood staining the white upholstery.

The black-and-white man instantly leaped for her still shapely figure, only to be blocked and pushed roughly back by the man in the leather mask. The big third man stared the other man down for a few seconds, then returned his attention to the girl.

Gingerly, almost gently, he removed the ropes from her body. She soon lay exhausted, but unbound, on the couch.

"There," said the old man. "That's perfect. It was all perfect. The brunette died on the hook. We chopped the boy up in front of her. The blond went through two windows. It's all working out beautifully!"

Ronnie understood his words, but not his meaning. The sense of dèjá vu had returned to almost choke her, but she didn't want to know the meaning of this insanity. Nor did she want to go insane.

"Come on," said the black-and-white man. "Put the blond kid in the chair. That'll stand in for the wheel chair."

The old man considered it, then nodded. "Okay," he said. They lifted Todd and plopped him into a padded white chair as the man in the leather mask went back into the kitchen.

"This is great, isn't it?" the black-and-white man asked the old man intently as he tried to bring Todd around

26

by slapping his face rhythmically. "I mean, it's working out great."

"Shut up, will you?" the old man ordered as Todd groaned and shifted uncomfortably in the chair. "He's coming around."

Ronnie watched it all from her prone position on the couch. She had long since stopped feeling anything except a weird chill across her entire body. It was as if she were totally buried in pure white snow that numbed her and made her sleepy. She watched the scene as if it were a movie. In fact, her mind told her in an analytical and matter-of-fact way, she had watched most of the evening's violence from the viewpoint of an audience. Even when some of the horror had gotten to her—as in the case of her father—she was still looking at the whole thing as a dramatic scene.

As if on cue, a sputtering roar came from the kitchen. The sound was like thousands of chattering demons and it was accompanied by a cloud of oily gray smoke which coiled out into the living room. The noise was enough to return the blond youth to full consciousness. He sat upright in the chair as the old man and the black-and-white man clamped down on his arms. He looked at both of them, vainly struggling and kicking, as the sizzling sound grew nearer. He twisted his head in the direction of the noise just as the man in the leather mask came out of the kitchen carrying a portable chain saw.

Ronnie had no mental defenses left to prevent the wash of déjà vu from completely flooding her brain. She knew exactly where it was coming from now. She had seen this before. The only difference between the scenes was that now she was viewing it clearly in reality. Before she had been watching fantasy between the fingers clutched to her face.

Todd had taken them to a movie. It was the greatest one, the one that started it all off—a real mind fucker—he said. Ronnie had seen the poster on the way in. It was not encouraging. There was a fat man with a strangely wavy face near a screaming brunette girl. The title on the poster was "The Texas Chainsaw Massacre."

For once, Todd had been right. The movie was a real mind fucker. It was nasty, bloody, and unmerciful—just like the three madmen who had invaded her home. She started remembering the specifics of the horror movie.

She remembered that near the beginning, a brunette was grabbed and smashed onto a hook which was hanging from the ceiling. Then her boyfriend had been dismembered before her dying eyes. Later a boy in a wheelchair had been sliced apart in a forest. And a pretty blond girl—a girl in a T-shirt and jeans—had been held captive, bound and gagged. In order to escape, she forced herself to leap out of two windows in the course of the film.

Ronnie pushed her gaze lazily back toward the kitchen. The man in the leather mask was coming around the plush white chair so that Todd could see him. Any noise the handsome boy made was drowned out by the ripping sound of the whirring chain saw. Ronnie saw her boyfriend's arm muscles and neck tendons bulging as he attempted to pull away from the other's imprisoning arms. But he wasn't going anywhere.

Ronnie knew what was coming. She let her head roll to the other side so she wouldn't have to see the worst of it. But her neck muscles reacted too slowly. Before she could look at the ceiling and then the back of the couch, she saw the spinning metal teeth of the machine sink into Todd's leg. She then knew that the reality of slaughter was more horrendous than any filmmaker's imagination.

The whirling steel links of the chain coughed up pieces of denim, spurts of blood, and bits of flesh. This time Todd's voice could be heard above the roar of the machine's engine. His scream seemed to reverberate throughout the house—enveloping all the other corpses in the kitchen and upstairs. Ronnie continued to hear his scream long after it had been choked out and only the noise of the chain saw remained.

The two smaller killers had let go of their blond male captive moments before and had stepped back to survey the third man's assault. After the mayhem aimed at Todd's leg, the man in the leather mask had drawn the saw across the youth's torso, then along his arm, then across his neck. Todd flopped and jerked in the now blood-covered seat as he felt his body being torn open and his innards gushed out. He felt as if he were caving in on himself—drowning in a sea of his own blood. Even after he lost consciousness, he probably felt the ripping pain until he died.

When Ronnie's head rolled back, the chain saw was still growling, but it was at the leather masked man's side. She saw all three men looking down at a twisted, pulpy crimson thing which used to be her boyfriend. They were staring at it dispassionately, but she could see the black-and-white man's eyes twinkling. Then, as she looked at them, they all turned to look back at her—as if they were all controlled by one mind.

She understood what was happening now. They were three madmen who had killed her parents, then decided to reenact "The Texas Chainsaw Massacre" movie with her and her friends. Brian, Todd, and Becky had each represented a different film victim. And she had been chosen as the heroine, the girl who remained their bound captive through some of the film, only to escape at the very end.

29

With this thought echoing in her almost demented mind, she viewed the killers' approach with inner calm. The heroine got away at the end, she remembered. The blond girl got out of their clutches and was picked up by a passing motor vehicle. So Ronnie looked at their blank, shiny faces without worry. She ignored their blood-caked weapons. In her addled brain, she felt certain that they could not harm her. She was the one who survived.

Her twisted thinking was confirmed for a split second when she heard the voice coming from behind the leather mask. Then there was nothing between her and instant insanity.

"You got away in the movie," the man in the leather mask told her. "But we're changing the ending." Then they fell upon her.

Ronnie spent her last moments on earth as an insane, dying girl. Considering what they did to her, it was better that she was not rational.

The sound of the grinding chain saw echoed through the house and out into the night.

Chapter Two

The grinding of the orange juice machine brought Brett Wallace back to reality. He snapped out of his depressive reverie to watch the juicer automatically put the squeeze on the bright, orange hemisphere the waitress had slipped inside its moon-shaped maw. From the little nozzle underneath came a spurt of orange, pulpy liquid, complete with pits. As soon as the grinding noise stopped, the waitress pulled open the machine's top, pulled out the crushed half orange, threw it away behind her in one fluid motion without looking back, and slipped another half inside. The moment she dropped the hinged top back on, the grinding process started again.

Brett couldn't help but smile. His sudden humor was not brought on by anticipation of the fresh orange juice, but by the casual professionalism of the waitress. She was a big, middle-aged woman with a masculine face and white hair arranged in a bun on the back of her head. She had reduced her waitressing to a science over the years, eliminating all unnecessary movement. She put in, and pulled out the orange halves, then threw them away perfectly—all without turning around and without missing the garbage can under the counter.

Wallace could appreciate her style and he enjoyed watching her. She did her job and nothing could faze her, not even the culinary changes that had been wrought in this diner. Originally it had been a truck stop exactly like thousands of other places all over the country. It was a shoebox with a double doorway in the middle of the side wall. On either side of the doorway were booths. Across from the doorway was a Formica counter which stretched across the opposite wall. In front of that were stools and in back of that was another counter lined with all the paraphernalia customarily associated with these diners. Directly across from the front doors were the kitchen doors. On either side of those were the glass-fronted dessert display case, the milk and iced tea dispensers, the coffee and hot chocolate makers, the milk shake mixer, and the fruit juicer.

As a regular diner, the establishment had been doing very poorly. It was located smack in the middle of Sausalito, near Bridgeway and Caledonia Streets. Not many truckers passed the place regularly and the hip citizens were getting their grub at places like the Venice Gourmet Deli, Soupcon, and the Trident. So three lawyers from San Francisco bought the place and got the bright idea of turning it into an Art Deco health food dinner. They just shined the place up a bit, got rid of the junk food and fired the cook. After shipping in fresh fruit, vegetables, and wheat germ, everything remained the same. Even the menus looked like classic diner material, only they listed entrees like salads and pita vegetarian burgers.

And since Brett Wallace was one who only put good food into his body, he decided to give the place a try. Especially since he needed some time to digest the horror he witnessed across town.

The waitress had filled a glass of the freshly squeezed yellow-orange liquid and was just about to pour the stuff into a strainer to get rid of the pits when Brett spoke up.

"I'll take it the way it is," he called quietly to her. He knew it might throw her practiced equilibrium off a little bit, but he didn't want to lose any of the orange pulp which would stick to the glass. He liked the pulp. At home, he'd probably eat most of the rind as well.

The waitress stopped in mid-movement, then slowly turned toward the medium-height, sandy-haired man sitting behind her, one eyebrow cocked in disbelief. She set the unstrained juice in front of him and asked, "You like pits, huh?"

Brett could see the beginning of a grin at one corner of her mouth. He should have known. With all her years behind the counter, she had probably seen everything.

"Yeah," he replied. "They're real crunchy."

"Okay," said the waitress quickly, "just don't make too much noise chewing. All right?" Then she was instantly off to another patron.

Brett smiled again. She had gotten in the last word and left before he could reply. She was a pro, all right, and a damn good waitress. She'd get a nice tip from him. He appreciated people who could roll with the punches without losing their style or dignity. Someone else might have given him a hard time about it.

Brett took a swig of juice. They used high quality oranges here so the liquid went down smoothly without the excess acid found in so many of the homogenized juices. And the pulp was rich and plentiful. It was just the refreshment he needed. Wallace swallowed and glanced around to look out the window at his car parked in front. The police uniform was on the floor between the front and back seats. He had brought it along just in case the somber, ill-fitting suit didn't work. Even though he had been sure that the gray, tweedy suit would make him look innocuous enough not to be noticed, he brought the uniform just to be on the safe side. The creed of the Ninja Master borrowed heavily from the Boy Scout code —"be prepared."

But just as he had thought, the fashionable mansion had been crawling with cops of all varieties—uniformed and plain clothed. And while there had been several curious bystanders in suits among the crowd outside, Brett altered his aura until he *was* a plainsclothes detective in thought and deed. He adjusted himself so perfectly that even if some other cop noticed him among the police army, they wouldn't think to question him. Brett had merely crossed the police lines, entered the house, surveyed the scene, and left—sick at heart.

The pulp in the glass in front of him had nothing on the pulp he had viewed at the Hansen mansion. There the pulp had been all red and was liberally draped on the floors, walls, and even the ceiling. As soon as Brett heard about the massacre of the family and some of the daughter's friends, he had gone to his wardrobe to put on the gray suit he had bought off the rack for this very purpose.

Brett's wardrobe had grown enormously in recent times. But rather than holding his street clothes—which he kept in drawers off to the side—the hangers held costumes and uniforms of almost countless varieties. The word "ninja" could be translated as "invisible" and Brett found that the best way to hide in a crowd is to become one of the crowd. So he had become a plainsclothes cop to investigate the murders of John, Patricia, and Veronica Hansen as well as the deaths of Todd Ingram, Brian Kelman, and Rebecca Osbourne.

What he had found in the living room and kitchen of the home nearly broke his concentration. The two rooms were a smoky, sodden slaughterhouse, filled with piles of drying crimson-gristled bone, and jagged-edged limbs. It was the scene of sadistic, violent debauchery of the worst kind. It had unavoidably reminded Brett of the murder scene that had confronted his eyes more than a decade ago—when his own wife and parents had been brutally murdered. It was then that he had set himself upon the road of vengeance—the road that led him to the ninja training and the mastery of deadly arts which made him the Ninja Master.

The eyes that took in Ronnie Hansen's devastated

corpse and the bodies of her friends and family were not the same eyes which had seen his own parents and beloved Kyoko dismembered. Although they were the same physically, these eyes held no horror or despair. These eyes already knew the depths to which humanity could sink. The only thing these eyes acknowledged as unusual was the ferocity of the attack juxtaposed against the quiet elegance of the surrounding. Mass murder was nothing new, the killing of the rich by the frustrated poor was nothing new, and the slaughter of innocents by crazy cults was nothing new. But in the more notorious cases there was always something a little warped about the victims.

In the most sensational case—that of a beautiful, pregnant actress and some friends butchered by a group of psychos while her director husband was out of the country—the victims led a very high life of drugs and sex. But in this case, the Hansens seemed the most civilized of families. There seemed to be nothing to mark them as targets other than the fact that they were rich. Brett mentally shrugged it off. Nowadays, no one needed an excuse to kill, so why was he looking for a motive? In his own case, his family's killers had just been some bikers hopped up on angel dust.

Brett left the mansion site to ruminate on what he had seen. After his family had been murdered and after his ninja training, he had vowed to assist anyone who had been as grievously wronged as he had been. Only here, there seemed to be no one to assist. If he followed up on these murders, he would be avenging the dead. The only reason he could see to find and punish the Hansen killers would be to prevent further tragedy and to right the lopsided scales of justice.

So Brett went to the health food diner to think about it. But once he had arrived and taken the first swig of orange juice, he found himself intent on not thinking about it. He found his mind wandering over the ramifications that his ninja training had on the rest of his life. He realized that he had subconsciously separated the pits from the pulp once the liquid was inside his mouth. His tongue had automatically pushed the white seeds into his cheek while his throat muscles swallowed the juice. Brett also realized how much better food tasted since his heightened awareness had flowered. He could distinguish tastes the way Sherlock Holmes could identify every tobacco simply from its ash.

Brett was now able to differentiate between such things as bland, sweet, and sour lettuce. He could tell how old the head was and where it came from simply by biting into one leaf. It was not something he worked at—it was simply something that *was,* thanks to his exhaustive training. As he was thinking about this, the waitress swept by, effortlessly dropping a salad plate in front of him even though she was carrying four other plates for the booth behind him. The waitress smiled as she was passing, knowing Brett was a nice guy and she was showing off for him.

Brett returned her smile as she rounded the edge of the counter and approached the booth. The booth held what looked to be four executive secretaries out for an early dinner after a hard day's work. Brett only saw them at the very edge of his peripheral vision, but he had them pegged as soon as they came in. He knew how tall they were and how much they weighed simply from listening to their footsteps as they had entered and walked toward the booth. Listening to them sit down gave him a good idea as to how each was shaped. Combining the sound of their breathing with the sound of their cloth covered rears rubbing against the plastic of the seat covering, he learned all he needed to know.

The final details were filled in with a single glance in their direction. One was overweight, but all were fairly attractive in the fresh-faced, tan, California manner. Their hair color ranged from bleached blond to black, with a lustrous auburn. It was the auburn hair that set the alarm off in Brett's brain. He had seen the hair before. Not just the same color hair, but specifically that hair. Wallace was too precise to make a mistake. Without looking back, Brett looked down into his salad and set his computer-like mind to work.

Lynn McDonald, he remembered. That was the beautiful girl who belonged to that hair. Brett didn't remember her so much as he remembered a feeling. A strange feeling that combined warmth and pleasure with pain and guilt. He remembered why he recalled that feeling so easily. She was the first woman he had been with after his first ninja mission, and the last woman he had seen before his invaluable retraining and ascent up the "Mountain of Fear" during his second mission. She had given him the warmth and pleasure, but he had felt the pain and guilt because he had yet to exorcize the horror of his family's death and the rage of his revenge.

His ninja teacher-senseis had finally eradicated the last vestiges of his destructive emotions, but his relationship with Lynn McDonald had been a victim of the change. He had not seen her since he had left Sausalito to destroy the neo-Nazi outpost on a mountain in Virginia. But coincidence had brought them together again. And as she sat behind him in the booth, he remembered her visage.

He remembered the tawny, wavy, hair cascading down

her ivory shoulders. And her body: soft and smooth while still muscular enough to hold her feminine shape in perfect proportion. He remembered her round, strong breasts, hardly bobbing beneath her silky shirts even without a bra, her long, curved legs, her small, well-shaped feet, her beautiful, rich, dark brown eyes, and her full red lips.

For a second, the indecisiveness, confusion, and frustration he felt before his retraining returned to him. But then he realized that it was only the memory of these feelings that had surfaced in his mind. He could no more feel these emotions again than he could forget how to breathe. He knew that he harbored no fear or doubt about seeing her again. At one time he thought that he would make himself all but invisible to her eyes if they met again, but now he knew he had nothing to regret or avoid.

"Excuse me," he heard a mellifluous voice behind him say. He remembered its richness clearly. It was her. He turned around on his stool easily. His vision swept by the rest of the restaurant until her face filled his vision. She was as lovely as before. As his eyes met hers, she audibly gasped, then cut the sound off. "It *is* you," she breathed in near disbelief. "Brett."

"Lynn," he replied, eliminating anything but the most pleasurable surprise from his voice. After his abrupt disappearance from her life, he didn't want her to feel anything but happiness at finding him again. "I just got back," he told her before she could think about how he hadn't written or called. "Please sit down. I must explain it to you."

His manner and voice was so open and earnest, the woman couldn't help but feel relief that he was in one piece, rather than anger that he had left her without a word. Besides, she considered herself a "modern girl," one who could take the various comings and goings of the men in her life in stride. But Brett, of course, was something special.

"What happened to you?" Lynn asked, suddenly wearing an expression of concern. "One day we had our usual dinner at the French Restaurant on Monday night and the next minute you disappear from the face of the earth." She pulled her small handbag strap from her shoulder as she settled onto the stool next to him, her back to the front doors. She ignored the intent, curious looks of her three companions. Suddenly there was nothing more important than what Brett had to say.

"It was family business," Brett told her honestly. "Very painful family business."

The look on Lynn's face told him that she remembered his telling her that he had been married and that his wife had died brutally. There was nothing wrong in him telling that to her or any other woman. It explained why he never brought up the subject of marriage. McDonald put her hand on his arm.

"I called and called your house, but no one answered," she informed him. "When I went there, I found out it was sold. Then, no matter how hard I looked, I couldn't find hide nor hair of you."

"I'm sorry," he answered. "But there was nothing I could do. I couldn't bring myself to call you. It wasn't the sort of thing I wanted to share. It would have been unfair to burden you with it." Oh, aren't I the cunning one, Brett thought to himself. With just a few words and an earnest manner, he had turned himself from a heel who deserted her to a sensitive man sparing her unnecessary pain. Furthermore, it made her feel all the more maternal toward him.

"Oh, Brett," she told him with deep feeling and conviction. "I'm sorry."

"It's over now," Brett told her, letting relief creep into his voice. "How are you?" he asked, switching subjects. He let his eyes take in her entire being. "You look wonderful." From anyone else it would have been a cliché, but from Brett's lips it had meaning. Lynn actually looked down at herself and blushed.

"I've missed you," she said quietly, volumes of meaning behind her words. She was wearing a classic woman executive's outfit consisting of a dark, V-necked pullover under a tailored white jacket and a tight, white slit skirt. High-heeled strap shoes that matched her shirt completed the picture except for chains around her neck and wrist. She looked better than wonderful. She looked spectacular.

"I missed *you*," he replied, honestly. Even though their words were the same, their meanings were different. She wanted him back, badly. He fondly remembered their times together, but knew that history could not repeat itself in his case. He would always miss her, but he couldn't chance her becoming serious about him again.

Given that Women's Lib had all but hurled male and female stereotypes into the abyss, that was all Lynn needed to hear. "Listen," she said. "I don't want to expose you to the vulgarities of 'dinner with the girls' and if I go back to them all they'll want to talk about is you. I also don't want to interrupt your meal—"

"Oh, listen—," Brett began, trying to diminish the importance of the salad.

"So why don't you put that in a doggy bag and join me for a more intimate supper somewhere else?" She ended her question with a smile that would have cut off any other man at the knees. It wasn't dazzling; it was insidiously effective. She merely looked down, then raised her clear, deep eyes until they were looking into his, all while the softest and smallest of smiles was on her lips. There was no way Brett could say no to that, even though he wanted to.

What he said instead was, "It's a deal."

Lynn rose from the stool triumphantly, her smile of seduction changed to one of glowing happiness and almost girlish anticipation. As she went over to the booth to bid some hasty farewells, Brett let all his worries drain out of him. Lynn was so beautifully and refreshingly alive that he couldn't help but feel a trifle glad that it worked out the way it did. Her energy and beauty would counteract the horror he had glimpsed at the Hansen house. He could convince her that their deep relationship was over later. First he'd have a good dinner and an entertaining evening with a woman worthy of his attention.

He spun back to the counter to drain the last of the orange juice. As he raised his head, he saw a reflection in the mirror behind the dessert rack. It was just a fleeting glimpse, but Brett's mind locked onto it like a 35mm camera. Even as the liquid moved down his throat, he wrenched his eyes off the ceiling and back to the reflection. There was a group of men. Brett instantly pegged their number at five. They were casually but neatly dressed in jeans and corduroys, with shirts and pullovers beneath windbreakers or baseball jackets. And they had unmistakable bulges in their pockets, the kind of bulges made only by guns.

It wasn't those bulges alone that made Brett believe he was in for trouble. It was the matter of their entrance and the look on their faces. Their expressions were set in determination and their skin was flushed with adrenalin-pumped blood. They entered like the front line of the

Green Bay Packers, spreading out as they moved past the door frame, their hands dug into their pockets for their weapons.

Wallace was frozen in place for a split second. Roaring through his brain was the realization that he was trapped. He knew instinctively that these men were not out to merely rob the place. They had murder written all over them. And normally Brett would have attacked devastatingly and escaped into the night—no one being able to give an accurate description of their lethal savior. Only this time there was someone who'd be able to provide a remarkably accurate description of him. And the cops would listen to her once she established that she had been his lover.

And once that was done, it was unlikely—but possible —that they'd connect her description with the sketchy descriptions of the man who had broken up a gang of black hoods, destroyed a southern neo-Nazi laboratory, eradicated a Mexican white slavery operation, and wiped out most of the Atlantic City mob. Even without matching up this fight with those feats, the cops would still be on the lookout for him, making it impossible for him to remain in the city.

Brett cursed to himself. He couldn't lay into these men the way he wanted to—the way it had become natural for him to. He had to stop them in a recognizably human fashion. He couldn't let anyone think that he was anything more than a very good fighter.

The first man inside pulled a .357 police Magnum from inside his jacket. He stood facing Brett while pointing the shiny, bracketed barrel at what seemed to be the most prominent target: Lynn McDonald. Instantly, before all the men were able to fan out, Brett put down his glass and scooped up his heavy porcelain salad plate in one movement. Without changing his position, he hurled it like a Frisbee at the first man's face. Only his strength and speed made the heavy, flat piece of china move about as fast as a cannonball.

The salad went spinning off in every direction, but the plate hit its mark at blurring speed. The edge wasn't sharp enough to slice the skin at the bridge of the man's nose, but it did break the skin and bone there before shattering into dozens of pieces which could cut with the best of blades. The man's head was thrown back and his face cut open, but Brett had not been fast enough. While he had been thinking about the predicament, the man had aimed and was already pulling the trigger. Brett had succeeded in throwing off his aim, but not in preventing the trigger being pulled.

The man leaped backward as the Magnum boomed. Lynn screamed and started at the sound. The bullet streaked past her and slammed into the chest of the girl nearest her in the booth. Her beige buttoned shirt suddenly sprouted a spitting rose from the right side of her chest and she jerked in her seat, her eyes wide. Then her head fell back to clunk on the top of the wooden booth seat and she died. Lynn stepped back, her hands over her mouth in shock.

Brett had been moving off his stool long before. The sound of the plate smashing and the gun blasting temporarily froze the other men's movements. The two men who had entered right behind the first man had split up. One, with a long-barreled .38 caliber police revolver, had run toward the other end of the diner to either cover or kill those sitting there. The other, hefting a .45 Army automatic, went for the kitchen to deal with the help.

As Brett came off his seat, his right hand went back and grabbed the stool under its lip. He moved forward, pulling the piece of furniture over his head as if throwing a spear. No one in the diner had any idea that his strength and control was better than even an Olympic athlete. All they saw was that the stool sliced through the air, seat first, to smash right into the face of the .38 man—like a pie splashed into Soupy Sales. But this harder surface didn't shatter like the plate. It depressed the .38 man's face into a flat surface. His nose was crushed and pushed inward and his lips were squashed before his head bounced back from the speeding stool. As the chair fell, the .38 man fell back and smacked the back of his head against the wall.

All the sounds of destruction brought the .45 man up short. As he turned, Brett vaulted over the counter and dropped on him, pushing his head back and slamming it on the top of the coffee maker. A sudden clang reverberated throughout the diner. In retaliation, the .45 man brought up his gun. Brett grabbed the man's wrist with one hand while holding his neck in the other. He pushed the gun hand back until it was right under the coffee spigot. Then he kicked upward, his toe pushing back the spigot. Steaming hot coffee poured out of the nozzle and onto the .45 man's hand.

The man screamed in closed-eye pain, his fingers smoking. His hand opened and the .45 clattered to the tile floor. Brett looked over his shoulder to see the last two men come fully into the restaurant. One held a .45 automatic just like the one the coffee-scalded man had dropped and the other held a long barreled .357 Magnum revolver. They looked like the devil's idea of "Starsky and Hutch."

Still holding the scalded man's neck and arm, Brett twisted around so the killer's body was between him and the last two psychos. It didn't make any difference to them. The final duo charged, shooting.

Brett instantly twisted his profile face forward. He watched one .45 bullet come plowing out of the scalded man's back. The man jerked in Brett's grip, but the bullet zipped past the Ninja Master's stomach and sank into the kitchen door. With a sudden, abrupt push, Wallace sent the dying, scalded man forward. The two final attackers were taken by surprise as the man they just dotted with bullets leaped toward them. The man with the .357 just managed to get out of the way by tripping and falling under the counter to Brett's left. The new .45 man met the dead .45 man head on. Both went backward onto the floor.

Brett skittered over to the .357 man, took a second to scoop up the automatic juicer and then bashed him over the head with it. At almost the same moment, he plucked the revolver out of the man's stunned grip. He didn't bother holding onto it. With any other group, he would've shouted, "hold it" and covered them until the police arrived, but he knew that this bunch was crazy. They'd shoot back, knowing that even if one of them was shot, the rest would perforate Brett's hide. And he wasn't going to shoot one of these guys as a defense, either. He couldn't take the chance that the police would make a big deal out of it. He couldn't chance any undue scrutiny.

Out of the corner of his eye, he saw the dessert display case's door open on the pudding side. He flipped the .357 up and in, and it disappeared under a wave of lumpy tapioca. At the same time, Brett propelled the flat of his hand up and under the .357 man's chin. Flesh smacked into flesh just as the second .45 man got out from under the corpse of the first one. The .357 man staggered back against the standing .45 killer. Brett's open-handed punch had pushed his jawbone against his skull, cutting the blood off from his brain for a second.

He blacked out while falling back. The rising .45 man held him up for a second, then Brett took care of the rest. He vaulted back over the counter and hit the unconscious .357 man in the chest with both feet, catapulting him over his fellow killer's hunched form and smashing him into the cash register stand. The register clicked open and flashed "No Sale" as the .357 man thudded to the floor.

Brett landed on his feet in front of the dazed .45 man. He stared at him for a second, then spun around, lifting his foot in a perfect backward karate kick. His heel swiped across the .45 man's face, spinning him around and back. Brett stopped facing the .45 man's back. He then planted his left foot and drove his right foot high into the man's back. The karate kick sent the second .45 man diving head first through the diner's glass door.

Brett came to rest facing Lynn and her companions. He saw his former love trying to stem the flow of blood from her friend's chest, crying all the while. His feeling for her slowed his reflexes down just enough so that the first .357 man could jump him from behind.

The man who Brett had smashed in the face with the plate fell across his back, pushing him forward. Brett could see the man's ruined face looming over his shoulder. He pivoted to shake free of the stumbling man, only to find this was what the man had wanted all along. He pushed past Brett, heading unsteadily toward Lynn.

Brett's full concentration returned to his fighting. He got himself back in gear just in time to hear the wobbly .38 man come behind him after the .357 man. Brett's lashing arm was delivered to the .38 man's face with a mingling of anger and surprise. When Brett hit someone with a stool or plate, he expected them to stay hit for more than fifteen seconds. He felt more than his forearm bash the side of the .38 man's head, pushing him against the counter where he did a cartwheel without hands over the obstruction and landed onto the floor.

Brett, in the meantime, kept his attention on the .357 man straining to get at Lynn. He moved forward just as the bleeding leader grabbed a knife from the booth's place setting and lifted it high over his head, thus forcing the women executives cowering back into the booth, screeching. But all of the .357 man's energy seemed to be concentrated on Lynn. He lumbered forward, like a scar-faced Frankenstein Monster at the woman, his feet sliding along the floor and the knife waving in the air.

Brett came up behind the zombie-like character, grabbed the wrist of the knife-wielding hand, swung in front of the killer, pivoted to the left, and pulled. He had executed a classic shoulder flip—the initial, elementary kind that is taught to almost everyone in the schoolyard, police academies, gyms, and dojos. Only Brett's version was a lot more powerful. The .357 man soared upside down over Brett's head, did a complete somersault over the counter and then dove headfirst through the glass dessert display case door and fell ear-deep into the rice pudding.

For a few seconds, the interior of the diner was deathly quiet. Gone were the gunshots, the shrieks of surprise and the shouts of confusion. Once Brett had sent the last killer through the display case, all the shocked patrons were hushed in appreciative awe.

Brett, himself, couldn't help feeling pleased. He had stopped the attackers without revealing his true abilities.

47

Lynn McDonald was safe. He felt bad over the death of the other girl, but he was thankful that no one else—except one of the gunmen—had been shot. The Ninja Master stood between the women's booth and the counter, his back to the main diner section.

Everyone remained stock still for a few moments to adjust to the silence. Then, before the patrons were able to react, three of the five attackers began to stir.

Brett heard it as a shuffling of glass at first. Even so, he could scarcely believe his ears. Wtihout turning his head, he looked to his left. The first .357 man was slowly extricating his torn head from the rice pudding, which was now completely mixed with blood. His eyes returned to the center as he heard the .38 man pulling himself up from behind the counter and the second .357 man rising from behind the cash register.

Then he heard the audible gasps of surprise from the rest of the patrons. They couldn't believe that they were seeing what Brett was hearing. Over their sounds of shock, Brett's sensitive ears picked up a further sound—a noise coming from outside. Brett's eyes moved in that direction just in time to see the man he had kicked through the door pulling a sawed-off shotgun out of the front seat of a Cutlass Supreme. Brett's hand lashed around Lynn's elbow. He pulled her down to the floor with a quick tug just as most of the glass in front of her exploded inward.

The screams started anew as the noise of the window blowing in mingled with the boom of the shotgun. Pieces of the pane fell on Brett's back as he shielded Lynn's body with his own. As soon as the worst was over he jumped to his feet, ready to take on the resilient killers. Only they didn't want to take him on anymore. Using the shotgun blast as cover, the three who could walk, did—toward the shattered front door.

Brett saw the last of them slip outside as he vaulted onto the booth table and then leaped out of the broken window. He landed on the hood of a car two autos down from the attackers' Cutlass. Having been beaten so badly, all had to leave their handguns inside the restaurant while the man with the shotgun had expended both barrels on the window. Left without a weapon and faced with what seemed like a living one, the men piled into the car, even as its engine was gunned into life.

Brett was steeling himself to take on the car when he heard the unmistakable wail of a police siren coming from around the far corner. The killers heard it too, hauling the Cutlass out of the parking space backward and pointing its nose in the opposite direction. In their haste to escape, they scraped off the back lights of the car parked next to theirs and bashed in their right fender.

Brett dropped to the left side of the car he was standing on as the Cutlass roared past—away from the oncoming siren. He saw the men pulling up more shotguns and rifles as they sped past him. He looked over his shoulder in time to see the cop car come screeching around the far corner, its gumballs blazing, bathing the street in red and blue light. Someone in the kitchen must've called the cavalry, Brett reasoned, while he was holding off the bad guys.

He took in the street scene quickly. The diner was on the south side of the road which stretched east and west for a good hundred yards. The two cars were about forty yards apart. As Brett calculated this, the killers' car suddenly bloomed gunfire. They had opened their remaining firepower on the pursuing vehicle. The police vehicle kept coming, while unleashing some bullets of its own.

Something in the back of Brett's mind told him to let the cops take it from there. Anything more from him might place him in a compromised position. But at the same time his hand was already snaking down toward his belt buckle. In his mind he pictured the dead girl in Lynn's booth and the rest of the terrified girls cut by the flying glass. After that, there was no way he was going to let the killers get away, even at the risk of revealing his half-secret identity.

The belt buckle was a simple, small, wooden rectangle. It was plain and innocuous, but it had a small metal holder on its back. Out of this Brett pulled what looked like the four-sided head of a spear. There were two long points on its east and west side, with two shorter, thicker points on its north and south. Crouching so that the parked car was shielding him from the cops' sight and his back was blocking the diner patrons' view of what he was doing, Brett held the sharp, small weapon in his palm. He had to move fast before the Cutlass got out of range.

Although the metal, handleless, throwing dirk was strong, it had the thickness of two razor blades. Held so that its side showed, it would be all but invisible. Because of its size, it was like throwing a four-pointed gold credit card. Brett's elbow bent as his eyes focused on the spinning right rear tire of the Cutlass. What his eyes saw locked into his brain and his arm straightened. He alone could hear the hum of the whirring weapon as it shot toward the car and see its shadowy golden trajectory as it buzzed through the air.

Luck was with him. Just before the spinning blades sunk into the heavy rubber of the wheel, the chasing cops let off a flurry of gunfire. The bullets ricocheted off the street and pumped into the cutlass trunk, but

Brett's four-sided steel star tore a wide slit in the tire. All the air inside burst out like a violent sneeze, sinking the right rear section of the auto. The Cutlass had just reached a getaway speed of fifty miles an hour when the tire blew.

The car swerved to the left, the driver too surprised to control the vehicle. The pursuing police car braked in response as the Cutlass body squealed and turned sideways on the street. Its weight and speed were too much for the three intact wheels to handle. The right front tire bent, then burst under the strain. There was no controlling the vehicle then. It seemed to lazily roll over onto its side, then pick up speed for a sudden one-and-a-half-rotation spin.

The auto smashed down on its other side, propelling it forward with another spin. It smashed back on its other side, then fell over onto its ceiling. The Cutlass slid down the remainder of the road, barely missing a car that appeared around the right-hand corner. That innocent car swerved and came to rest on the empty sidewalk. The few remaining pedestrians on the street flattened themselves against the walls and sidewalks, everyone else having gotten off the strife-filled roadway when the first gunshot sounded.

Brett was satisfied. He had stopped the killers so the police could mop them up. He was just about to turn back toward the diner when the Cutlass Supreme blew up.

The detonation and concussion didn't shake him up as much as the realization that even with a full tank of gas and even if an errant bullet had hit it, it was extremely unlikely—despite what TV detective shows presented—that the car would explode. And certainly not with this fireball's rage and power. Brett was pressed back against the car he had been leaning on by the shock wave. When he could look at the wreck clearly he could see that most of the flames were concentrated on the car's underside—which was now facing the night sky.

The police car had screeched to a halt halfway down the street and the two cops inside were too busy calling for assistance to do much right away. And when they did get out of the car, Brett assumed they would be more interested in safeguarding innocent bystanders than seeing if any killer was still alive.

Brett ran into the street toward the flaming wreck. The fire billowed up, allowing Brett to get close enough to see inside. He could see movement through the heat haze and the crushed, broken windowpane and frame. Brett got as close as he could without his hair being singed to see one of the men crawling across the still bodies of the three others. He saw the cut and bleeding man struggling to grab something. As Brett watched, the last survivor pulled up another small shotgun. Then the Ninja Master and the killer's eyes met.

Brett was astonished to see the man smile, revealing half a tongue and chipped teeth. The man's head started to nod as if he were soundlessly laughing. Then the man put the barrel of the weapon next to his head and pulled the trigger.

He was still smiling, his head nodding, when his brains erupted out of his left ear.

Chapter Three

The image of the silently laughing, exploding head stayed with Brett Wallace even in the hospital. When he wasn't thinking about that, he had the mental picture of three men who should have stayed down rising slowly inside the health food diner. And when he couldn't avoid it, he remembered the terribly sad look Lynn McDonald gave him when he finally came back inside the restaurant.

Her white suit was streaked with the blood of her writhing, wounded friends. She was trying to soothe and treat all of them at once when Brett pulled open the smashed door and walked in. For a split second she looked right at him, her expression mingling horror, guilt, pain, and blame. She felt the guilt—irrationally thinking that her desire to desert them brought on the attack. And she blamed him just as irrationally—first, for making her want to leave her friends, and second, for saving her and not them.

There wasn't a cut on Lynn, but one of her friends was dead and the other three were severely slashed by flying glass. Brett felt no guilt, but he did feel frustration and confusion. The attack on the diner had come out of nowhere and made absolutely no sense. For some strange reason, the attackers seemed fixated on Lynn McDonald. The .357 man shot at her first, then went at her with a knife, and the man outside blew apart the window in front of her with a shotgun. Brett could see no reason why they were so intent on killing her other than that she was the most beautiful and noticeable person in the place.

Perhaps the head man had a one-track mind and, once Brett had thrown his aim off, focused on eliminating his original target. That reasoning was valid, but Brett couldn't buy it somehow. The insanity and intensity of the attack made him feel that there was more to it than met the eye.

"Mister—" said a male voice above him and to his right. "Wallace?"

Brett looked up at an overweight, short, balding man in a three-piece suit holding a clip board. "Yes?" he asked by way of reply.

"Good," the man answered, plopping down next to him. He then shifted his grip on the clipboard and held out a pudgy hand. "I'm Lieutenant Anthony, Sausalito homicide."

Brett took the offered hand. Anthony had a strong grip and Wallace felt muscle beneath the heavy rolls of fat around the police officer's fingers.

"Thanks for waiting," he continued, becoming engrossed with the facts on his clipboard. Once the ambulances had arrived at the diner, Brett and Lynn had been whisked away in the company of the overweight girl who suffered cuts on one side of her face. On the way to the hospital, a police sergeant had taken their names, addresses, and stories. This information was what Anthony was skimming, no doubt. It took longer than usual because the lieutenant's eyes were bloodshot and bleary.

Finally he blinked, and looked back at Brett. "Everything seems perfectly clear," he said with a wan smile.

"Given the circumstances you did an extraordinarily brave and stupid thing. It's just very lucky for you that things didn't turn out worse."

"Those men were going to shoot up the place," Brett told him quietly. "They shot that girl in cold blood. I had to do something or I would have been killed too."

Anthony's eyes narrowed and his lips pursed for a second. Then he set the clipboard down between them with a wide, forced smile. "You're a pretty good fighter, by all accounts," he said. "You know a little kung fu, huh?" The lieutenant jabbed his hands out in succession in a bad impersonation of Bruce Lee.

"I work out," Brett said agreeably. "I took some Tae Kwon Doe in college. I still do the exercises."

"Humph," said the police man. "Well, it's all pretty cut and dried. There's been corroborating eyewitness evidence to your claim of self-defense and it's clear that you didn't shoot the alleged assailant found dead outside the kitchen."

"Any identification on him yet?" Brett asked.

Anthony eyed him, unable to keep suspicion out of his expression. He paused as if considering whether or not to give Brett a hard time, then replied in the negative.

"Nothing," he said. "Yet. The car was stolen and they had nothing in their pockets but guns."

"Any way to trace them?"

"You kidding?" Anthony snorted. What he couldn't understand was why he was talking so openly with a man who was supposed to be a suspect. "The guns had their numbers filed off and even if we were able to find the salesman, the weapons probably went through more hands than a Spanish whore during a fiesta."

Brett knew why the cop was so gregarious. It was the combination of exhaustion brought on by too big a case

55

load, and Brett's professional attitude. He was still in the plainclothesman suit and still sending off police vibrations. Because the lieutenant was so tired, he felt as if he were sitting down with one of his peers for a bull session.

"Naw," he continued. "We'll check the files and send out a picture of the guy who was shot, but I doubt if we'll get any sort of response. Even the people who knew him are probably happy he's croaked and out of their life. The rest of the guys—well, there's not enough left of them to identify."

"Pretty rough," Brett commiserated.

"You ain't kidding," Anthony replied, rubbing his eyes. "Things are bad enough with this Hansen thing, and now this had to happen. They're pushing for a quick wrap-up on this one upstairs. Just a bunch of hopped-up assholes out for a little action who get out of control. They see a good-looking broad in the diner window and decide to blow her away to prove their male superiority. Some fucking world, huh?"

"You buy that?" Brett asked.

"Looks like I don't have a choice," Anthony complained. "It closes the file and nobody has any extra time to do any special digging. They kill a woman, they get killed in return. An eye for an eye. Justice is served. Nobody in my department is going to make waves on this one."

"Yeah," Brett agreed. "It's some world, all right." He decided to push his hand a bit. "Any progress with the Hansen case?"

"Shit," spat Anthony, leaning back on the hospital couch, his eyes closed. "Less than nothing. You'd think that anyone leaving that much of a mess would leave some kind of clue, wouldn't you? We got plenty of bloody footprints, but no fingerprints. They took all the weapons with them. It'll take a week just to wade through all the blood." Anthony's eyes suddenly popped open and his expression said that he realized he had been saying things only his peers should hear. The police tradition was to tell the public less than nothing. But looking at Brett assuaged his consternation. Brett made his face say that Anthony could trust him implicitly. Even more, it said that Brett understood perfectly everything Anthony said. Everything about Brett said to the cop that he was "one of them."

"Good luck with it, man," Brett said. "It sounds like a bitch."

"Aren't they all?" Anthony snorted, getting up. He pushed the clipboard under his arm and looked down at Brett for a couple of seconds, bemused confusion on his face. Then he shrugged minutely. "You're all right, Wallace," he judged aloud. "Stay out of trouble. And if you can't stay out of trouble, take care of it yourself."

He started back toward the intensive care unit. Brett stopped him. "What about the girl, McDonald?"

Anthony stopped and turned his head back. "What about her?"

"Can I see her?"

Anthony looked down at his clipboard. "Her friends were treated and released. We let her go with them. She left the hospital ten minutes ago."

Brett immediately got to his feet. He swallowed his sudden anger, realizing that, at this stage of the game, it wouldn't even occur to Anthony to inform Wallace of Lynn's departure. He had more important things on his mind.

The lieutenant wasn't too busy to snort at what he saw as Brett's sudden macho protective instinct. "Don't worry about her, Wallace," he advised with a grin. "She can take care of herself. Besides," he continued, "she saw enough action tonight to last her a lifetime. Give her a chance to get over it before you see her again. And take it easy. Lightning doesn't strike twice in the same place."

The trio of killers parked the car a block away from the house and walked around to the back. Opening the trunk, they found everything they needed inside: three pairs of black gloves, three black telephone cords, three hard plastic masks depicting a blank, youthful face, and three long, wide, sharp kitchen knives.

The trio picked up the masks first. Two of them slipped on the disguises easily, but the third, fat man couldn't get the rigid neck piece over his big head. He threw the mask back into the trunk with disgust, then walked to the front seat to grab his leather one. While there, he reached over the seat to retrieve his black bag full of handcuffs and knotted strips of cloth.

Then all three trudged casually to the white, two-story, well-lit suburban house comfortably nestled on two acres of precisely manicured grass. Thanks to the gathering darkness outside, they could see in, but the people inside could not see out. One of the men in the blank-faced masks licked his lips. Even that could not be seen because these flesh-colored faces only had holes for the eyes and nostrils. Everything else was obscured by pale plastic.

Inside the house, Jenny Curtis had her hands full with the Beymer twins. The two young boys were making too much of a racket for her and her friends to study. Besides, they were supposed to be in bed watching television. It was only out of the kindness of her heart that she let them watch the evening movie in the first place. That, and their sworn promise that they would sit and watch it quietly in the privacy of their own room.

Jenny excused herself, got off the couch, and marched up the stairs to the boys' room. She flung open the door to find them swatting each other over the head with their pillows in the dark interior—lit only by the bluish light of the black-and-white TV.

"All right, that's enough!" Jenny cried, in her best authoritarian baby-sitter voice. Both boys stopped in mid-swing, more than a little annoyed at the interruption, but well aware that Jenny had the power of siccing their father on them when he got home. "I thought you said you'd be quiet," she admonished.

"Aw, gee, Jenny," Geoffrey complained. "It's no good up here! Can't we come down to the living room and watch it in color?"

"No!" she declared.

"Just one part?" Daniel pleaded. "It'll only take a couple of minutes."

"No," Jenny repeated.

"But it's really great," Geoffrey declared. "This acid rain comes down, y'know, and everybody starts melting, like."

"It's really neat," Daniel stressed.

"I said no!" Jenny punctuated the conversation. "You're just lucky I don't switch off the set here and now. If you don't just lie there and watch quietly, you know what'll happen."

"Aw, shit," Geoffrey whined, dropping his pillow behind him and settling down on his haunches. Daniel hissed as a warning in case his brother didn't notice he just swore.

"You better hope I don't tell your father about that," Jenny warned.

Geoffrey grumbled.

"What?" Jenny inquired.

"All right," Geoffrey grunted. "We'll watch quietly."

"That's better," said Jenny, then left the room, closing the door behind her.

"Geez," said Daniel, slightly in awe of his older brother.

Geoffrey shook his head, then leaned back with his hands between his hair and the pillow. "For such a cute girl," he declared, "she can be an awful bitch."

Jenny lightly hopped down the stairs and apologized to Karen and Linda. "A baby-sitter's work is never done," she shrugged.

"Well, come on, already," said the bespectacled Karen. "I didn't even start on half of this stuff and we've got to know it by tomorrow." The girl had dirty blond hair, freckles, and a voice that sounded like a cross between a Muppet and a smoke-detector alarm.

"Take it easy, will you?" said the more sophisticated brunette, Linda. "It's not like we've got a surprise quiz or anything." She was more casual than Karen, who was wearing a loose dress. Linda was wearing a one-piece swimsuit and cut-offs.

"You never know," Karen intoned, intent on her books.

Jenny sat down on an armchair across from the couch and picked up a book from the side table while curling her denim-covered legs beneath her. She pushed her straight black hair away from either side of her face in order to see her studies unobstructed. "Okay," she said brightly. "Where were we?"

Before either of her friends could reply, they were interrupted by the blare of the upstairs television. It filled the L-shaped combination living and dining room with the cries of the melting damned trying to escape the "Devil's Rain."

Linda groaned and threw her book down. Karen looked around the room, confused. Jenny snapped her book shut. "I knew I shouldn't have let them watch that movie," she said. "They're really going to get it this time," she vowed, getting up and dropping her book on the seat.

"Let them have it!" Linda called to her with glee as she mounted the stairs again.

"Do you need any help?" Karen yelled after her.

"No, thanks," Jenny shouted back over the din of the film's sound-track. She was going to handle the spoiled little monsters herself. She got up to the second-story landing all set to fling open the door and tear into the kids like she never had before. She was going to give them a piece of her mind they'd always remember and then she'd tell their father to take a piece out of them that they'd never forget.

Jenny let her anger drive her to their door. She grabbed the doorknob as if she was going to arm-wrestle it, then hurled open the obstruction. She was ready to give it to them—but the two side-by-side beds were empty.

The wrinkled sheets were illuminated by the glow from the TV screen. For a moment, Jenny was taken by surprise, but then she figured that the little bastards were playing a game with her. They turned the sound all the way up to get her back for a session of hide and go seek.

"Okay, you creeps," she said under her breath. "You're asking for it." She reached over and flicked up the light switch. The overhead lamp did not go on. She smirked. Trust the cunning little devils to unscrew the bulbs, she thought. This little charade was going to end tragically, she promised herself. But she certainly couldn't think about what to do next with the television that loud. Stepping carefully, she moved up behind the set, reached around, and turned the volume down.

It was from that angle that she saw the small figure above the closet door. With a nerve-shocking start, she realized that it was the form of Daniel Beymer, stuck eight feet up the wall like some sort of baby Spider Man. His feet were resting on the top of the closet door frame with his knees bent. His hands were at his side and his head was down—his chin resting against his chest. There was a round shadow and a dark line coming down his front. The shadow of the round shape in the middle of his torso cut his wide-eyed face in half.

In silent amazement, Jenny moved around the TV table and over toward the closet. She prayed that she'd trip over some Beymer-created booby trap and the kids would yell surprise, but it didn't happen. She was almost crying in fear when she reached the side wall. From that angle she could see that Daniel was pinned to the wall by a large kitchen knife which protruded from his chest.

She screamed once, sharply, just before she heard the door downstairs crack and swing open. Then the tail end of her scream mingled with those of her friends downstairs. Jenny choked off the rest of her shriek, her hands clutching the lower part of her face. She looked wildly around the room for any sign of Geoffrey, but could find none. Just then, she heard Linda scream for help, followed by laughter and a strange kind of choked burbling.

Her terror propelled Jenny out of the boys' room and down the hall toward the master bedroom. She threw open the door and leaped for the Princess phone on the side table. She lifted the receiver but the automatic light on the dial did not go on. She held the receiver to her ear, but there was no sound.

She choked back another cry and turned toward the door. There stood three men holding her two friends. The first man was holding Karen up by a telephone cord wrapped around her throat. Karen's eyes were closed and her tongue was bulging out of her mouth. She hung down, motionless. Linda was struggling in the grip of the second man, her hands cuffed behind her, cut-off shorts taken off, and the man's gloved hand over her mouth. The third man held a head in his hands, a head that looked exactly like the faces of the men holding the other girls. Only this head was glowing with a strange, yellow flickering as if it had a candle inside. It looked like a jack-o'-lantern on Halloween.

This time Jenny tried to scream, only no sound would come out. Her mouth opened and closed, but she could only hear the sound of her breath catching in her throat. She made no more noise than a cricket. Jenny dropped the phone as two of the men moved forward. She moved back as the first man threw Karen onto the bed. Jenny, petrified by fear, stayed still, next to the bureau as the other man set the glowing head down beside the useless phone.

After doing that, he looked at Jenny, bathed by the eerie light of the human-shaped ornament. He was a big, overweight man wearing a mask made out of leather. Seeing him full face forced Jenny to act. She tried to slip by him, but he pushed out one large paw which she ran right into. Suddenly his arm was around her waist and he was pulling her toward his girth. She managed to scream again, only to have a wad of knotted cloth pushed deep into her mouth.

All her energy was concentrated on not choking. But by the time she managed to get the cloth away from her tonsils, another cloth had been tied around her head and the big man held her arms at her sides. The men holding both girls watched, seemingly calm, as the third man produced another kitchen knife and held it over Karen's motionless neck. He looked through his mask at his twin in the doorway and at the fat leather masked man by the bureau. Each held a squirming teenager in his grip. Both nodded slightly. The man looked back at Karen and slit her throat with the knife.

Dozens of alarms and sirens went off in Jenny's mind. They blinded and deafened her. In the corner of her mind, she thought she heard Linda wailing, but then, just like the wail of a ambulance speeding past, the noise diminished. When she could see again, the bedroom doorway was empty.

Unfortunately the bed was not. Karen was still there and blood was gushing out of the slit in her neck. It splashed the covers, the phone, and the lamp. Some blood dropped over the bed's edge and onto the carpet. That was the last Jenny saw of her friend. The big man pulled her out of the room and dragged her down the hall, back to the twins' room. Inside, more horror awaited.

Linda was lying on her back and cuffed hands atop one of the boys' bed. Her bathing suit was still on, but it had been cut open at the crotch and pulled down off her shoulders. One of the men with the masks was on top of her, while the other held Linda's legs apart. The big man holding Jenny seemed to ignore the scene, opting instead to tromp over to the closet and pull the door open beneath the corpse of Daniel.

Inside the closet, Geoffrey Beymer hung by his knees from the cross bar. His arms were hanging toward the floor, his eyes were closed and his Underoos had a crater in the middle of his chest. The big man let go of Jenny with one arm and pushed the boy so that he swung back and forth on the bar. Then he threw Jenny to the floor of the closet.

She hit the boards and rolled to the corner of the enclosure. She pulled herself into a little ball, her hands up to protect her face. Instead of screaming, she was gasping for breath—beginning to hyperventilate. The big man pulled the knife out of the boy above him. The corpse fell to the floor with a sickening thud. The big man then turned to his associates.

"Come on," he said. "The target will be home soon."

"In a second," said the quickly grinding man on top of Linda. "In a second," he repeated, picking up speed. "In a second, in a second, in a second, in a second . . . !" As his movements became more pronounced and he picked up more and more speed, he held his knife closer and closer to Linda's chest. Suddenly he sighed, stopped and plunged the blade between the girl's breasts.

Jenny heard her friend's death rattle even over in the closet. Then all three men appeared in the doorway. Each held a kitchen knife in his hand. All three were bloodstained.

"You got away in the movie," said the big man to the baby-sitter. "But there's no one to save you now."

Jenny remembered the glowing jack-o'-lantern head in the bedroom before all three men took turns stabbing her.

Mr. and Mrs. Beymer saw nothing out of the ordinary as they drove up to the house after having their weekly bridge night and dinner party with friends. As they moved up the walk, Mrs. Beymer noticed that the front door seemed different somehow. She shrugged it off, thinking that the twins had just slammed it once too often. She went up the stone steps first, eager to say hello to the girls and make something for them in the kitchen.

As she turned the knob and entered, her mouth opening to say hello, a .38 caliber bullet entered her left ear and imbedded itself deep within her brain. She never knew how or why she died. She didn't even feel herself fall over and hit the floor heavily.

All Mr. Beymer heard was a cough and soft thudding sound. "Are you all right?" he asked his already dead wife as he entered and before he saw her prone body. The door was pulled out of his grip and thrown wide as hands grabbed his shirt front and threw him to the floor. He rolled and stopped in a sitting position. He looked up into the barrels of three silenced pistols. Then an inky black fist lined with red hit him in the face. The fist spread after it connected until it covered his entire head. Then his body numbed and started to float. Distantly he heard that same cough multiplied three times. Then he heard and saw and felt nothing more.

The three blades hurtled toward Brett Wallace's chest. He stood before them, his entire body exposed to their speeding points. He only moved just when they seemed destined to sink into his flesh. Then both hands shot up as his body dipped so fast the movement seemed invisible. The back of one hand slapped the side of one knife. The side of his other hand hit the flat of the other blade. The third knife's path was unobstructed, but it did not reach its target. Its target moved so that the third blade sunk into the wooden partition behind Brett—between his shoulder and neck. The first two knives smashed into the wood wall on either side of the Ninja Master's head.

"Bravo!" said Jeff Archer appreciatively, being the man who threw the knives. He clapped his hands together twice, using applause as a method to dispel his own tension. It was never easy for him to try to kill his Master, even when the Master demanded it. And although Brett had diverted the blades, he was still depending on Archer to throw them perfectly straight. Jeff worked hard to make sure the knives didn't wobble at all in midair. Just because his teacher was the Ninja Master didn't mean he knew everything automatically. Part of being the Ninja Master was learning new things all the time. And in Brett's case, that meant learning the hard way.

"All right," the Ninja Master said to his student, who was ten years younger than him and also happened to be a teacher of black belts. "Let's try spinning them now."

"Spinning?" Archer asked incredulously.

"Most street fighters couldn't throw a straight knife if they wanted to," Brett explained. "Their knives are usually of the switchblade or hunting variety, which usually wobble or spin in the air." He waved both hands in a "come on" motion. "So throw some spinners."

Archer raised an eyebrow at the request, but sighed and shrugged as he turned his attention to the wealth of different knives on the table next to him. The table stood at one end of Brett's cavernous training room beneath the Dawn Dojo—the martial arts studio Wallace had bestowed on the twenty-five-year-old Archer upon the former's return from the Orient. Upstairs, Jeff taught more than a half dozen classes in the skills of weaponless warfare as well as the art of the art. To pass Archer's test, his students must also be as well versed in the wonders of the mind as they were in the violent capabilities of the body.

Downstairs was what could be termed Brett Wallace's "Batcave." Like it or not, he had made himself into some sort of "super hero," utilizing much the same approach as the fictitious comic book Batman. The one thing he had over the cartoon character, however, was a dozen years of special training in Japan's ninja school. The one thing Batman had over him was that the Caped Crusader's fights weren't for real. There was no way a fictitious character could get killed, unless his author did it. Brett wasn't so lucky. He was master of his own fate.

Jeff plucked up two hunting knives and a switchblade. He laid the hilts of one hunting knife and the switchblade in one hand, then held the second hunting knife with the other. Brett stood, seemingly unconcerned, thirty feet away from him. His hands were at his side and his eyes were narrowed. Archer superimposed a cross-hair sight on his teacher's face, pivoted, raised both hands, then brought the arm down. All three knives spun forward, almost like the four-edged dirk Brett had sent spinning after the diner attackers' car.

Almost, but not quite. Archer did not have the speed or expertise his Master did. To Jeff's surprise, Brett moved forward, toward the oncoming blades. His hands went up and his head whipped around in a blur of flesh. Suddenly the knives were no longer spinning, but they weren't stuck in the wood partition behind Wallace either. In one hand Brett held the first hunting knife by the hilt. In the other he held the second knife by the blade. The handle of the switchblade was in his teeth.

Archer's jaw dropped in shocked respect. It was an act that Lieutenant Anthony might call extraordinarily brave and stupid. Especially since Brett then grimaced and threw the hunting knives down. There was a thin cut across his palm from the blade he caught. Archer ran up to him as Wallace spit out the switchblade.

"Damn," Brett cursed quietly, looking at his injured hand.

Archer took Brett's arm in his own two hands, and examined the palm like a seasoned medic. "It's not very deep," he reported, at the same time realizing that Brett was too good a martial artist to let it go very deep. "Naturally," Jeff added. "Even so, it should be bleeding a lot more."

"It's all in the mind," Brett explained with a smirk. "I've slowed my heart and pulse rate. It won't start bleeding in earnest until I let things go back to normal. What say you to bandaging it before that happens?"

Jeff looked up in surprise. Sarcasm wasn't one of Wallace's strong suits. The look on his face didn't jibe either. It was about the first time Jeff had ever seen Brett with a sardonic expression. Archer immediately went over to the bathroom to retrieve the medical kit without questioning his teacher. Only after he had tended to the cut did he cautiously bring the subject up.

"Anything wrong?" he casually inquired, putting the Ace bandage clip in place. Brett looked at the flesh-colored covering wrapped around his palm with unusual interest.

"You bet," he finally answered with humor. Borrowing the words of Lynn McDonald, he continued. "Why don't you and I have an intimate dinner someplace and discuss it?"

It had been two days since the Hansen House Massacre (as the crime was labeled). Ronnie and her family had died late one evening. The next afternoon Brett had visited the catastrophic scene only to waltz right into the middle of another massacre at the diner. The ramifications of that kept him up most of the night and the following morning. Now it was one night later and Brett's view of the world had not improved. He kept seeing Lynn McDonald's tortured face and the face of the laughing, bloody man who blew himself away before he could be captured or immolated.

But while Brett was trying to adjust to this, the world kept turning and things did not get better. In fact, once Brett and Archer arrived at the Rhea Dawn—the Oriental restaurant owned by Rhea Tagashi where Brett was a "silent partner"—reality had taken a distinct turn for the worse. The two men went up the side entrance to Wallace's special dining nook located just above the main dining room, and to the right of the kitchen. The last meal had been served an hour ago and the help was presently washing the place down.

The two men went upstairs to Brett's loft living area to find Rhea and her cook, Hama, sitting around the highly polished wooden table, watching TV. The television was all the way across the room, located in the center of Brett's massive entertainment and home computer center. Almost all the components were supplied by Nippon Electric—a Japanese firm which specialized in the most advanced gadgetry available on the market.

Although that area gleamed with metal and plastic, the rest of Brett's home away from home was decorated in the simplest and most elegant of Oriental taste. The news that screamed across the airwaves seemed out of place in the civilized surroundings.

"At first the Hansen House Massacre appeared to be an isolated incident," the black female reporter intoned, "but now a second mass murder of an entire family has rocked the area. In what is being called the 'Beymer Butchery,' the four members of the Beymer family in Marin County have been discovered brutally killed. For more on this story, we go to Nick Miller on the scene. Nick?"

Brett watched as the picture shifted to a calm-looking suburban house bathed in television lights and surrounded by an army of police and reporters. In the foreground was a dapper young man holding a microphone with one hand and his ear with the other.

"This peaceful, well-tended street seems to be the perfect example of the American Dream," the reporter started. "But early this evening, inside the house you see behind me, that dream turned into a nightmare."

Hama snorted at the consciously melodramatic prose.

"Mr. William Beymer had called Jennifer Curtis, a local high school honors student, to baby-sit his twin sons, Daniel and Geoffrey, while he and his wife, Dorothy, went to a friend's house for dinner. According to our reports, Jennifer refused to baby-sit unless she could have two friends come over to help her study. Mr. Beymer agreed to that request. That decision cost Jennifer, and two of her girl friends . . ." The reporter checked a paper in front of him. ". . . Karen Palmer and Linda Evanston, their lives."

Brett sat down, his back to the set. "Turn it off," he said irritably.

Rhea, wearing a kimono top over her wrap dress, looked at Wallace in surprise. Brett had his head in his hands, seemingly tired. The long-haired Oriental woman frowned, but pressed the "off" button on the remote control box. The reporter's face and voice faded out. Rhea noticed Brett's bandaged hand immediately.

"We don't have all the details yet," was among the last thing they heard the TV reporter say, "but we'll keep you informed of things as they happen . . ."

Jeff and Hama made little noises of discomfort and irritation as they shifted in their seats away from the set.

"You notice how the media has to give a catchy name to every murder and killer?" Archer sarcastically inquired. " 'The Boston Strangler,' 'The Hillside Strangler,' 'Son of Sam,' and all the others."

"Yeah," said Hama, his bald pate still glistening from

the sweat he worked up making all the Far Eastern delights in the kitchen. "And they'll be interrupting every show tonight with the gory details no matter if its a sitcom, or what. You also notice how they never have those special reports during commercials."

"Enough already," Brett interrupted. "What happened?" he asked Rhea tiredly. The other three looked at each other as Wallace continued to cover the top part of his head with his hands. This was unusual behavior coming from Brett. Still, they trusted him too much to question him immediately.

"Seven people killed," Rhea told him. "Three high school girls. Two small boys. And the parents of the children. Shot, stabbed, and strangled.—So far, there's been no distinction between who was killed how. There may be some evidence of rape as well."

"Well, at least that leaves the boy victims out," Hama said with relief, never really enjoying these body counts. Although he was the weapons expert of the team, Hama felt a lot more comfortable with killing machines than he did with the victims of those same things.

"In this crazy world, you can never be sure," said Brett, finally lowering his hands. He put them palms down, flat, on the table. "Any real connection between this and the Hansen House murders?"

"No way of telling," Rhea reported. "The press is having a field day, of course."

"Of course," Jeff interrupted with disgust.

"And while they've spent a lot of hot air about the intrinsic violence of our society, the general consensus is that the killings are unrelated to but inspired by the Hansen Massacre."

"It's incredible," Hama added, shaking his head. "The TV news people come off shaking their heads in amazement that the public would be so interested in these deaths as if they had nothing to do with it."

"You going to look for yourself?" Archer inquired.

Brett leaned back in his chair, looking over Archer's head out the tall bay windows across the room. "No," he finally said. "I don't think so."

"Brett," Rhea interjected. "What happened to your hand?"

Brett looked at his cut palm, seemingly seeing through the Ace bandage, and smiled. He decided to answer everyone's question at once. "Too much thinking. Too little concentration," he started. Then he told them about encountering Lynn McDonald and the diner attack.

"I heard about that," Hama said with surprise. "The news reported it as a simple robbery and police shoot out. Your name wasn't mentioned."

"I made sure of that," Brett replied.

"Could it have anything to do with the Hansen massacre?" Rhea inquired. "Could someone have seen you at the house and decided you were dangerous?"

"I doubt it," Brett said without pride. "These men seemed completely uninterested in me. All their concentration seemed to be on the girl."

"Then why attack a diner with five guys?" Jeff asked. "There seem to be a lot more practical ways to kill one girl rather than sending an army into a restaurant."

"One man stood in the center of the place and pointed his gun right at her while the others fanned out," Brett mused. "No one fired their own weapon while this first man was aiming. They all seemed honestly surprised when I interrupted and deflected the shot. Like they couldn't do their own killing until the first man downed his target.

"Could you be making more of this than you should because of the girl?" Rhea asked, unable to quell just the smallest bit of jealousy, but keeping Brett's slashed hand in mind.

Wallace smiled with understanding at her across the table. "You know better than that," he said quietly. Then his face became distant and concerned. "But she shouldn't have left the hospital so quickly. It wasn't like her to leave without at least seeing me."

All three of Brett's associates were worried now. Wallace was acting less than objective about the whole thing. They couldn't tell how much of Brett's concern came from hurt ego and how much stemmed from his investigative abilities.

"She was frightened," Jeff suggested. "It must have been quite a shock to be attacked like that."

Brett turned to his student and partner. "She was frightened, all right," he said with conviction. "But the fear of attack should have been over. All the men who attacked the diner were dead. Why would she keep running?"

"Not everyone is a ninja," Hama contended, his arms out. "Not everyone can just shrug off something like that."

Brett did not rise to the bait. Rather than countering angrily or defensively, he rose from the table and walked toward the computer, his hands behind his back. All three remaining seated looked at each other with expressions of surprise and concern.

"It's been a long day," Rhea finally forced herself to say. "And it looks like an even longer one tomorrow. I think we better get ready for it."

Hama and Archer took the hint. With some uncomfortable clichés, they made their farewells and took off. Rhea slipped off her kimono and approached Brett, putting her hands on his shoulders. To her surprise, he didn't need a back rub. His muscles were completely relaxed.

"That was awkward, wasn't it?" he laughed, referring to the hasty exit.

Rhea had stopped being surprised at Brett's shifts in personality long ago. She took his sudden humor in stride. "They're not used to you like this," she said. "And to tell you the truth, neither am I."

"The past has caught up to me," Brett explained, more seriously.

"You can't just leave it behind," Rhea soothed him. "We all knew this kind of thing could happen."

"I was much too visible when I first got back from Japan," he agreed. "But no one knows this woman the way I do. She wouldn't just leave the hospital and run scared if there wasn't a reason."

Talk of Lynn McDonald didn't faze Rhea. She kept her arms around Wallace. "It's been a while since you saw her before last night," she offered as explanation. "Contrary to popular belief, people can change enormously in a short amount of time. You're living proof of that."

Brett shook his head. "Something's wrong."

Rhea let him go and walked in front of him to the simple seat in front of the TV system. "It's obvious that you're not going to let this thing go until your conscience is satisfied. And until you get it out of your mind, you're not going to be able to put your attention on things like this Hansen and Beymer killings."

"So?" Brett asked, bemused.

"So go see her," Rhea suggested. "Come to some kind of understanding with yourself. Either renew your relationship or end it for good. At least it won't be preying on your mind after that."

Brett had to admit her logic was sound. His memory

of Lynn was chewing at the edges of his brain. He had to acknowledge that his interest was created by more than just the diner attack. He was still attracted to the girl. He remembered her address from when she gave it to the policeman in the ambulance on the way to the hospital. His internal sense of time told him it was close to midnight. Looking at the digital clock on one of his videotape machines, he saw that it was 11:39 P.M. Late, but not too late.

"All right," he agreed with Rhea. "Good idea."

Lynn McDonald's dwelling was a second-floor apartment in a reconverted mansion on Russian Hill in San Francisco. The place looked positively gothic outlined against the dark blue night sky. That image was enhanced by the one light shining in the window on the first floor. Brett parked his car across and down the street from the place. Getting out, he adjusted his gray slacks and dark blue shirt. The night chill did not affect him unduly—he rarely found need for a jacket in the temperate California climate.

Walking up the street, he noticed how empty and quiet it was. Even he could remember a time when the sidewalks would have been full of young lovers and others looking for love. People wouldn't think twice about walking home from a dance or the movies or dinner. But now people locked themselves in at night, afraid of anything that walked the streets.

And senseless murder was not confined to the streets. Once upon a time, people would get angry, maybe throw a few things, steam a little, then kiss and make up. Now it seemed like everyone had a gun in the house, they'd get angry, pull the damn thing out of the bureau and shoot each other. More than fifty percent of all homicides stemmed from arguments. And if that didn't

76

happen, then a gang would be lording over the street or a drunk would be weaving down the highway or a psycho would be waiting in the shadows. And all this was in addition to the rapists and professional muggers in the alleys.

"It's a beautiful day in the neighborhood," Brett sang the theme of the children's show "Mister Rogers" as he approached Lynn McDonald's place. He shook off all pessimistic thoughts to concentrate on his immediate surroundings. Lynn had given her apartment number as "2B," which meant it was on the second floor. Brett could see no lights on in the front. It could be that her rooms were in the back, he reasoned. He spied a thin, dark sidewalk on the side of the house and walked around until he stood in the near black alley behind the manse.

The moonlight gave depth to the rear of the building, so Brett could see some pale curtains blowing in the night winds. They billowed outward from an open sliding door on a second-story balcony. There was no light coming from inside. Brett moved forward, his senses alert. The weather was too cool for Lynn to have the windows open for comfort while she slept, and Brett couldn't think of any other good reason for the sliding door to be open.

He was halfway to the back of the building when he stopped himself. You're overreacting, he told himself with a conscious effort to relax. You're expecting the worst so you're creating the worst in your own mind. There didn't have to be a reason for the door to be open other than whoever lived there wanted it open. All the death Brett had seen and heard about and caused was getting to him, he decided. He purposefully stopped moving and turned his head to the side to laugh it off.

Then he froze. His nostrils flared. His head moved

easily from side to side. His eyes closed for a second and his mouth opened slightly. He smelled it. It was something he had smelled before, in far greater quantities. He had smelled it inside the Hansen house, he had smelled it in the health food diner, and he had smelled it in Sausalito, Virginia, and Atlantic City, New Jersey. Here the smell was indistinct and tiny, but it was there nevertheless. It was the stench of death.

Brett Wallace took two steps forward. He looked down. There was a cat's head lying in the alley.

Chapter Four

The cat's green-gold eyes were open and reflecting back what little moonlight there was. Its orange fur ended at its neck, which was matted in red blood, while some of its guts and brains laid out on the concrete beside it. There was a splotch of blood three feet closer to the apartment house, apparently where it had bounced after a long fall.

It took Brett one step to reach the spot and another step to get the speed he wanted, then his knees bent, straightened, and he flew upward. His body shot past the first floor windows. His hand grabbed the bottom of the fire escape and he pulled himself up until the soles of his shoes were flat on the fire escape railing. Then he straightened his legs once more and was hurtling upward again. His hands gripped the banister of the second-floor balcony even as his body continued up. He pulled so that he somersaulted onto the balcony floor.

When he landed, he continued his downward movement so that he somersaulted again into the apartment proper. As he came up, his ears detected no other movement in the flat and his nose pinpointed another death smell. His head swung in that direction. The rest of the cat lay in the middle of the room.

By the looks of it, someone had simply grabbed the pet and yanked its head off. The head was casually hurled out the open sliding door and the body just dropped. There was now a pool of blood and guts where the cat's head had been.

The casual cruelty here matched the enormous sadism Brett had seen evidence of at the Hansen house. He felt sure that the incident there, here, and at the Beymers were the work of the same sort of psycho. At the same time he was thinking this, he experienced a sinking sensation in his stomach. According to all his senses there was no other living creature in the apartment besides himself. He may have already been too late to save Lynn from whatever fate some unknown killer had chosen for her.

Silently and quickly, Brett moved through all the apartment's rooms. He found no one in his search, but did find enough evidence that the place was inhabited by Lynn. There were dresses he recognized in the closet in addition to some well-tailored nurse's uniforms. Her handbag was on a chair. Inside was her wallet complete with money, credit cards, and a clip-on nurse's i.d. Lynn McDonald had lived here, but Brett had to wonder whether she was living any longer.

His head snapped around as he heard something he determined came from three stories down. Since the building was only two stories, the sound had to have come from the basement. The noise had cut through the background sounds of a radio on this floor and a TV on the first. It was the sound of a muffled yell of surprise.

The sound had been choked off, and now, only with great concentration, could Brett hear a distant bleating. The Ninja Master ran back onto the balcony and jumped over the edge. He fell and hit the ground on his feet. He cushioned the shock of landing by dropping and rolling back toward the building. As he rolled, he spied a small cellar window blocked by two iron bars secured vertically. He stopped himself in front of these bars. As he had hoped, they were all but rusted away. With two vicious swipes of his hand, he broke them from their chipped concrete mooring and threw them aside. Without pausing, he pulled his body around, kicked through the smokey, opaque glass and dropped down into the cellar hallway.

He stood at the end of the hall which had three doors, one on each of the other walls. The one to his left led to a flight of stairs. The one on the right led to the laundry room. The one on the opposite wall led to the furnace room which Brett could see over four struggling figures. In the laundry room doorway stood a young, red-headed man choking a young girl with both hands while banging her head against the doorframe. Beyond him was a wiry, tall, white-haired old woman who was dragging the barely conscious form of Lynn McDonald.

Both attacking figures stopped in their tracks when Brett entered. As soon as they saw him, however, they only took a second to look at each other before they moved into action again. The redhead pushed the girl in front of him, wrenching her arm behind her back and burying a clutching hand deep into her hair.

"I'll kill her!" he shouted as the old woman continued to drag Lynn toward the open furnace room door. "I'll kill her if you don't stop me!" He shook the girl so that she jiggled like a doll in front of Brett. Her free hand was drifting between her waist and head, the pain he was creating making it impossible for her to resist.

Brett moved forward a step. The young man pulled the girl back a step. The old woman ignored it all, continually sliding Lynn across the floor as fast as she could.

"Yeah," said the youth. "That's it. Come on. Save this girl if you can." He began to turn the crying girl into the laundry room. "Come on, let me see you."

Brett moved forward quickly, his body leaning toward Lynn and the old woman.

"No!" the boy screamed, shaking the girl again. His movement was so abrupt, it twisted the girl's arm higher and nearly ripped out her hair. She cried out in pain. "Leave the lady alone. I'll kill this girl if you get any closer to the old woman!"

Brett stood in the middle of the hallway, amazed. Through the laundry doorway he could see the youth pulling the girl toward a line of four dryers on the far wall. One of the dryers was spinning a load of wash. At the other end of the hall, Brett could see the old woman dragging Lynn's body across the furnace room threshold. For a moment, Brett seemed to be stymied. It seemed that no matter what happened, one of the girls was going to die.

As he looked back into the laundry room, he saw out of the corner of his eye the old woman drop Lynn and swing the furnace room's door shut with a clang. As Brett's head turned in that direction he heard the door's locking bolt slam into place.

"Don't try it!" the redhead shouted. "Don't even think it or this girl dies!"

Brett remembered what his hesitation in the diner had led to. With a scowl, he started to charge into the laundry room. But when he looked at the redhead and his captive again, the boy was holding a snub-nose revolver to her head. He was backed all the way against the spinning dryer.

"Just stay there, man," the redhead warned. "Just stay right there or I'll kill the girl." Then he smiled as if he'd won a prize.

Brett glanced up without moving his head. The ceiling was crisscrossed with thick white piping. He saw one especially large pipe hissing steam at its junction over the dryers. Without hesitation, Brett leaped up, his arms rising above his head like spears. He heard the kid shout and then he felt his fingers digging through the thick padded cardboard insulation and the thin, hot metal inside. As he reached the apex of his jump, he pulled his arms forward, ripping out a section of the pipe's underside.

He felt heat scalding his hands and then he was falling in a cloud of hot, stinging steam. The heavy white cloud billowed out to engulf the youth and his captive as well. Brett landed on his feet as he heard the boy shout in rage. Thankfully he also didn't hear a gunshot. He remained still on the floor and closed his eyes. He used his other senses to pinpoint the lad's position. He heard where the youth had moved to and he knew he held the girl in front of him. Brett decided to act while the steam was still thick.

Silently he walked over until he was three feet in front of the angry, shouting redhead. Without opening his eyes to the scalding mist, his right hand lashed out, passed right next to the girl's head, gathered up the revolver and pushed it into the redhead's face.

As far as the kid could tell, he had just hit himself in the face with his own gun. He let go of the girl's hair in surprise. Then he hit himself again. He heard his nose crack and felt a rush of liquid course out of his nose and down his lips and chin. He fell back against the side of the spinning dryer. He moved the gun away from his face, only to feel it swing against the lip of the dryer, which suddenly opened—seemingly by itself.

Then the dryer door closed again on the redhead's wrist. It cut through the skin and nearly sliced the vein beneath. The kid cried out and dropped the gun like a hot potato. Right after his scream, Brett slammed the kid across the jaw with the back of his hand. It spun the boy around until he was in front of the open dryer. Brett moved over and kicked the boy in the chest with the side of his right foot. The redhead shot back, banging his head on the back of the still turning dryer. Brett bent the kid's knees and bundled his legs inside after him. With the kid completely inside the dryer, Brett closed the door and let the machine begin to spin again.

He moved quickly to where the girl was lying, gently helped her up to her feet and led her out of the room, swinging the door shut behind him. Only then did he open his eyes. The girl was kneeling on the floor, crying. The furnace room door was still bolted shut. Brett realized the heater would be working on this cool night.

He ran toward the metal door while shouting at the girl to call the police. He smashed into the obstruction, only to bounce back. The door was thick, heavy metal, not like the pipe in the laundry room, and the wall around it was unchipped reinforced concrete, unlike the cellar window he had broken through. Brett knew that time was not on his side. The old woman had been in there several seconds and his initial attack had warned her that he had gotten past the redhead.

Brett instantly attacked the door where it was the most vulnerable; the bolts and securing pins. Concentrating all his strength in the kung fu style he chopped at the right edge of the door until he felt the bolt rip out of the furnace room wall. He kept chopping down the length of the door until it started to give—the screws holding the door clasps pulling out of their concrete foundation. Brett felt the door wobble and move in.

He stepped back and kicked out with all his might. The top of the door fell forward into the furnace room, while one lone screw held the partition in the frame. Brett moved forward and swiped the metal door aside, the screw popping out of the wall like a BB shot from a rifle. The top tip of the door slammed down onto the floor, sending it cartwheeling across the dusty cement floor. Brett stood in the doorway, rage masking his face.

The sound of the door crashing in froze the woman in her tracks. She already had the furnace door open and Lynn McDonald's head halfway in. When she snapped around to see Brett, she dropped the younger woman's head. It hit the edge of the furnace opening with a sickening crack. Brett charged into the room as Lynn's beautiful auburn hair began to sizzle and burn.

An animal-like growl rose from his throat as his arms reached forward to crush the old woman. But she was too fast, even for him. Just as his fingers were about to touch her skin, she ducked down and threw herself into the furnace, laughing.

Brett slammed against the furnace, shock replacing the anger on his face. He looked down to see the old woman's foot snake into the furnace over Lynn's head. Brett lifted McDonald up and pulled her away from the heat. He tore off his shirt and wrapped it around her smoking head to smother the flames. When he brought the shirt up, her hair no longer burned and blood was soaking the underside of the garment.

Brett looked up in disbelief, his mouth wide. The door of the furnace was still open. Inside was the old woman, her face a crater of flame, sitting amid the fire. Her outfit had disintegrated, her hair had burned off, her skin was black and flaking, and her eyes were flaming pits. About the only thing left were her teeth. Her lips were black, curling ash, but the shape they formed was unmistakable. The woman was smiling in death. She had been laughing while dying. Brett could still hear the unearthly cackling reverberating through the room.

Brett forced his attention back to the girl. Her eyes were closed and she was breathing erratically. He felt a gash on the side of her head where the old woman had dropped her. Her scalp had been seared by the heat. Brett wadded up his shirt and used it as a bandage for the nasty cut. Then he touched many nerve points on her body utilizing accupressure. This too was part of the ninja art, but in this case, it did not work. No matter how hard he pressed and where, she did not awaken. Brett stopped, satisfied that the technique at least made her breathing regular again. He managed a grim smile.

The redhead landed screaming atop his head.

Brett was taken completely by surprise. Later he would remember being obliquely aware of the footsteps behind him, but his subconscious had told him it was the grateful girl returning to tell him she had called the police. Instead, it was the redheaded kid, flailing and scratching like a madman.

Brett fell over and shot his arm out, the elbow catching the redhead in the mouth. His screeching stopped and he dropped backwards. Brett rolled and got to his feet to face the youth—who also had found his footing. The redhead's skin was now the color of his hair. It was horribly scalded and scratched—in some places puffed up with a black circle around the wound. He had tumbled in that hot dryer for minutes, his flesh getting seared every time it touched the metal.

The two men faced each other across the furnace room for a second, then the young man moved toward Lynn's body. Brett, enraged and distraught, stepped into his path and delivered a devastating closed-fist blow to the jaw with all his enraged power behind it.

The first connected with the left side of the kid's jaw and kept going. The bone Brett's fingers contacted was crushed into meal. The right side of the jawbone tore off from the skull and ripped out the skin. The redhead literally spun in the air and then slammed into the wall face first.

Incredibly, he was still standing. Slowly, painfully—his arms moving like someone during an epileptic seizure—the kid turned back toward Brett. His face was now completely destroyed. His nose was bent at an unnatural angle. Blood was cascading over his lower lip like a waterfall. But still he stood. And a second later, even more incredibly, he turned and ran.

Brett was immediately after him, steeling his mind to the nearly superhuman strength and stamina these killers displayed. He followed the bleeding redhead into the laundry room. The kid ran right for the open dryer. He fell onto its lip, his back to Brett. He hunched there, his feet unsteady on the floor. Brett heard a sizzling as he approached the boy. Just as he got his hands on the redhead's shoulders, the back of the kid's head exploded.

Brett spun away as pieces of the kid's scalp flew up in a small shower of blood. Brett heard the bullet clatter a second later. He stood to the side and watched the kid slide stomach-first against the dryer bottom, then roll onto his back on the floor.

The redhead couldn't open his mouth after Brett had mashed it, so he had merely picked up his snub-nose and pointed it in the general direction of his head before he pulled the trigger. He must have been looking down the barrel, Brett realized, since his left eye was gone.

The Ninja Master could not say he wasn't shaken. He had seen dozens of people go down before his blades and fists, but he had never faced an enemy so intent on killing themselves before he did it. They were mocking him with their deaths, putting themselves out of Brett's reach.

Brett's attention was brought back to the real world when he heard the sound of sirens approaching the apartment house. When the police came roaring in, they found Brett kneeling over Lynn, still trying to stem the flow of blood from the gash in her temple.

"Call Lieutenant Anthony," Brett instructed the uniformed cops. "Tell him the diner attack was no fluke."

Brett felt completely naked. He was back in the hospital again, sitting on the same couch with the tired lieutenant. He had little choice but to be there. If he had run, the girl he had saved would have described him. Normally that wouldn't help the cops much, but this time Anthony had seen both him and Lynn. If he had run, the cop would have had to wonder why.

His first inclination as a ninja was to run. He remembered what his teachers had told him. "A ninja is not seen. He allows himself to be seen." And most especially he remembered the words, "an exposed ninja is not a ninja at all. He is a dead man." Brett would have to be very careful not to make one wrong step. He had to be especially careful because he was planning to make a lot of steps. He was going to keep stepping until he reached the reason why so many people seemed to want Lynn McDonald dead.

"She's in a coma," Lieutenant Anthony told Brett quietly. "I'm sorry."

Brett was wearing a hospital shirt since his own was ruined by Lynn's blood. "I'm just sorry I didn't get there sooner," he said.

"And what?" Anthony piped up. "Get shot when they caught you by surprise? You got there at the perfect time. You got the drop on them. You were just lucky you got your hands on the kid's gun."

"Yeah," drawled Brett, letting misery creep into his voice.

"Let's go through it again," Anthony suggested. "You say that they were already beating on the girl when you came in?"

"Right," answered Brett, exhaling. "The furnace door was already broken in. I didn't notice the broken window until after. What I can't understand is how they did it."

"The bars on the window were loose," Anthony tiredly surmised, "and they probably used a hunk of pipe from the laundry room to pry the furnace door off its hinges."

"Then how was it locked from the inside?" Brett wondered, the picture of innocence.

"I don't know," Anthony groaned. "Maybe McDonald locked herself in. You said you didn't see her when you got there."

"No," Brett agreed, letting Anthony assume just what he wanted him to assume. "I just saw the girl getting beaten by the redheaded kid."

"So you chased him into the laundry room, which was full of steam and got your hands on the gun . . ."

"I couldn't see a fucking thing, so I just turned it around, grabbed his head and kept firing until it was empty," Brett said, knowing that he actually blew the kid's face apart at close range after he heard the sirens, so no one could tell that he had pushed his jaw out of his head with one punch.

"That was a little extreme," Anthony interjected.

"What would you do?" Wallace growled. "I told you I couldn't see! All I knew was that kid had the girl!"

"All right, okay, take it easy," Anthony soothed, his hands out. "I can understand why you had to do it. What happened then?"

"I got the girl out of the room and told her to call the police. Then I ran in the furnace room. McDonald was on the floor and the woman was inside. I pulled Lynn away from the furnace and then your people arrived."

Anthony sighed, leaned back and thought about it a minute. "McDonald was probably stronger," he reasoned aloud. "The old woman was trying to pull her in, but the girl pushed. The woman slipped, McDonald hit her head and that was that." Brett looked at the cop with pain in his eyes. "Sorry," the cop added, realizing how flippant it sounded.

Brett looked away, his eye catching the nurse's desk. He saw an abrupt movement as he looked down the hall. A pretty blond nurse had been staring at him. When he looked over, she quietly busied herself at the desk. He slowly looked over at Anthony again.

"God," he almost whispered. "What am I going to do now?"

Anthony put his hand on Brett's shoulder. "Don't worry about it," he suggested. "It's pretty clear that you killed the kid in self-defense. The girl you saved isn't making much sense, but one thing she made clear is that you saved her. You may only have to sign a statement to that effect and it probably won't even come to trial. Not with the court schedules the way they are. And even if it does, you won't hear about it for another few years. You got a good lawyer?"

Brett nodded.

"Well, as soon as we identify the kid, you should get your man onto researching his family. The one way they can fuck you up is to sue you. Maybe you'll luck out. Maybe he'll be an orphan."

Brett looked up in surprise. "You mean you don't know who he is, yet?" Anthony shook his head. "What about his fingerprints?"

Anthony waved the fingers of his own right hand. "He didn't have any. They were burned off by acid."

Brett allowed himself to look confused.

"The mark of a professional," Anthony said. "Or a crazy person. They sear off the top layer of skin so they can't be identified."

Brett quickly looked back at the nurse's desk. The same blond girl was staring at him. Their eyes met and then the nurse tried to make believe that she was looking at him by purest chance. Her eyes wandered, then returned to him, and then she smiled bravely. Brett turned to face Anthony once more. The lieutenant misread Wallace's look of concern.

"Look, I told you not to worry about it, okay? You've proven to us that McDonald's life is in danger. There'll be a round-the-clock guard on her room, right? Just in case there are any more nuts rattling around the woodwork. And you've proven to them that you can take care of yourself. I pity anybody who's going to mess with you."

Brett fixed Anthony with a serious, probing gaze. "You don't buy it, do you?" Brett asked pointedly.

Anthony fidgeted for a second before replying. "You want the truth?" Brett nodded. "Okay," Anthony retorted. "No, I don't. Not completely. I don't think there's any conspiracy against your girl friend. I just think that McDonald is one unlucky woman. Listen, when whole families are being wiped out for no reason at all, and then the friends of the family are raped and murdered, well, it doesn't take much of an imagination to believe that one woman would get attacked twice in two days."

The lieutenant suddenly leaned in. "Hey, you know that movie 'Ms. 45?'" Brett looked quizzically at the cop, then shook his head no. "Well, it was based on a true story," Anthony went on. "This girl got attacked once at her place of business, once on the way home, and then another rapist was waiting for her inside her apartment. In the movie she went crazy and starting shooting any guy who came on to her. But in real life, she just went crazy. A vegetable, you know? She hasn't talked in four years. She's still down on the farm."

"The farm?" Brett echoed.

"The funny farm," Anthony explained. "And when I see that, I can believe that a bunch of guys are going to shoot up the restaurant she was in, and then a day later, some redheaded asshole goes nuts in her cellar."

Anthony was getting more and more worked up as he talked, but when he noticed passersby looking at him strangely, he calmed down with a visible effort.

"Ah, shit," he said quietly. "I haven't been thinking about your girl at all. I'm sorry, Wallace, but things'll turn out okay. The doc says McDonald'll probably come out of it. He says her heart is strong and her breathing's steady."

Brett looked at the floor. "I just wish I was there sooner."

"Hell, you saved her life," Anthony repeated as he got up. He looked at his watch. "Jesus, I got to go. We got a meeting with the Marin County cops on this Beymer thing. Take it easy, Wallace, and don't worry." Anthony left the couch and walked quickly down the hall. As before, he couldn't understand why he blabbed so much in Wallace's presence. There was something extremely personable about the man as well as something extremely strange. He seemed to ooze a superiority that made Anthony want to impress him or gain his respect. The cop shook the feeling off. Wallace was small change compared to the Hansen case.

Brett watched him go. The conversation had gone just as he wanted it to. He had used all his ninja mental arts to divert attention away from himself. He knew enough about psychology to know that the girl wouldn't remember many specifics about her ordeal and if he let Anthony come up with his own theory—rather than force one on him—the theory would stick. But Brett was not out of hot water yet.

He put his hands together and laced his fingers together, moving up to the edge of his seat and bowing his head as if praying. Then he looked to his right with only his eyes. The blond nurse was staring at him. She was not looking at him as if he were a patient to be pitied. She was not looking at him like a handsome man who might be available. She was looking at him as if he were an obstruction on a road she definitely wanted to travel.

Brett rose from his seat, turned his back on the nurse's station and walked out of the hospital.

Nurse Claire Dearborne left the supply closet at four o'clock in the morning, carrying the silver tray with the hidden syringe on it. Folded under the small pan on the tray was the doctor's order for a bed bath. Nurse Dearborne walked slowly and carefully toward her destination, allowing her shapely legs some freedom of movement under her short dress. She looked down at herself to make sure her zipper was open enough down the front so anyone over five-feet-six could look down her shirt.

She all but sashayed up to room seven-fifteen and the cop who sat outside. The policeman visibly brightened at her approach. He had gone through every magazine in the waiting room during his guarding shift. He had started with the month-old copies of *Time* and *Newsweek*, progressed to wrinkled, coverless *McCall's*, medical journals, and finally he was forced to peruse *Highlights*, the monthly for children which always had a cartoon character saying "Hello!" on the front cover and "Good-bye!" on the back.

He was so happy to see her knees above her shapely calves in the white hose, her waist between slim hips, and her well-endowed breasts (that appeared to overflow her shiny bra), that he hardly noticed the doctor's order and what it entailed. All he knew was that this nurse he had admired earlier had finally come to him as a blond-haloed vision to break the boredom of this mundane job.

She got inside the room as easily as could be expected considering the cop wanted to ravage her right there.

The difficult part was veering his attention away from *her,* not the syringe or bed-bath order. She managed to put him off by explaining that the cleaning had to be done before a certain time and by promising that she would be back later to chat.

She closed the door behind her, effectively cutting off all the light from the hallway. The room was dark, except for the light that came in from the windows, which created a dark blue glow around the bed in the middle of the otherwise empty room. On the bed, on her back, with tubes up her arms, nose, and mouth, lay Lynn McDonald. Wires had been stuck onto her forehead, neck, and chest. The bed sheet was folded over her stomach and under her arms. She lay, breathing peacefully, her eyes closed, while little machines beeped and hummed on the table next to her. Those dimly lit screens highlighted her still lovely face.

Claire Dearborne approached the bed with a smirk on her face. *Well,* she thought to herself. *You've been asking for it, sweetheart, and now you're going to get it.* She placed the tray on the table across from the respiratory machines and swabbed the top of Lynn's elbow joint with a cotton ball soaked in alcohol. The smell tickled Claire's nostrils. She lifted the syringe up to the moonlight and tested the flow. A thin stream of liquid arced up and then splashed down on the floor.

So far, so good, she thought. She took one last look at Lynn's serene face. Claire decided that she wouldn't mind McDonald being dead. It would just mean more money and power for her. And she didn't mind one less competitor for the doctors' attention. She leaned over, gripped Lynn's elbow with her free hand and set the needle's point at the comatose girl's vein.

She just started to press when the needle broke.

She started and gasped as the needle snapped upward at her. She dropped the syringe on the bed and stepped back, her hands over her mouth. She just stared at the bed a while longer, trying to slow her racing heart.

It was just an accident, she argued reasonably with herself. *You're just tense because you've never killed anyone before. But it's easy. Just inject her like you've injected dozens of people before and leave. Take off your uniform, get in your street clothes, and walk away. The guard was so busy looking at your tits, he won't be able to describe your face. Besides there were thousands of pert, blue-eyed blonds in California. So just relax and get it over with.*

By the time Claire returned to the bedside, she had almost convinced herself that the needle had broken as a result of her own clumsiness. She picked up a small, thin wrapper from the tray containing two new needles. She picked it open and removed one. With experienced hands, she removed the broken needle and replaced it with the sharp, shiny new one.

She was getting nervous again, she realized. She was taking too long to make the injection. The cop outside might get lonely and look in. If he saw her shooting McDonald up, he might shoot her up. At the very best, she'd be detained for questioning. And if that happened she'd be good as dead.

The nurse lifted the syringe with its new needle up to the window light. As soon as she pressed the plunger to test it, the second needle broke. It just dropped off, cut in half, while a tiny cloud of fluid splashed onto the pillow next to Lynn's head.

Claire continued to hold the syringe up, staring at it in

wonder. It just wasn't her night, she decided with a combination of toughness and stridency. Quickly, without thinking about it further, she pulled the second broken needle out of the syringe and groped for the third and last one.

"If this one doesn't work," she whispered to herself, "I'm screwed."

She got it all set up, then stuck it into McDonald's vein without testing it. Then she exerted pressure on the plunger. Nothing happened. The plunger did not go down and the deadly liquid did not drain out into Lynn's vein. Dearborne tried pushing it again. The plunger wouldn't budge. Sweating and looking around wildly, she exerted all the pressure she could on the plunger. But it didn't work.

In frustration and desperation she pulled the syringe out of the sleeping girl's arm and held it up to the window for examination. At that second a hand slid over her mouth and her fingers on the plunger were slammed upward.

The blow to her syringe hand was incredible. She felt a sudden strange pressure but no pain. This pressure had a strength that she could not muster in her whole body. It was enough to slam the plunger all the way to the syringe hilt. There was a soggy pop followed by a ting and a splash. She cried out in surprise but the sound was silenced by the gagging hand.

Then, just as fast as she was attacked, she was released. She rocked in place for a second, unsure as to what had happened. Then she looked at the syringe in her hand. The plunger was all the way down, the liquid was gone, and the needle was nowhere to be seen. Then she sensed a glint upwards and, raising her eyeballs, saw the needle sticking in the ceiling.

"You're screwed," said a small voice right in her left ear.

She spun around, totally petrified, expecting to see the policeman. She saw nothing . . . no one. She heard a sound behind her and whirled again—expecting to see McDonald sitting up in bed, eyes open, fingers pointing accusingly.

Instead she saw the comatose girl still resting and the room the way it had been. Except for one thing. Claire's eyes narrowed. There was a darkness blocking some of the moonlight streaming through the window in front of her. It didn't look like a solid blackness, rather the blackness one "saw" with your eyes closed or in a pitch-black room. In the center of this blackness was a thin, silver line. It was the silver than a bright light made while shining through the thinnest of cracks.

She gaped breathlessly as the shining silver line began to widen. It stretched out until it became a wickedly sharp, curved blade about two feet long. It was the blade of a samurai sword, floating three feet in the air in front of her.

Before she could move away, before she could shout, the blade disappeared again. She saw a small silver object taking an oval course through the air and returning to where it had been. Then she heard a tinkling sound below and looked at the floor. Between her white shoes was half the third syringe needle. She looked up. The other half was still stuck into the ceiling.

Claire Dearborne nearly fainted. She suddenly realized that the same sword had silently, invisibly, cut the previous two needles in half. And whatever could make a sword move that fast or accurately was something she didn't want to mess with. The nurse left everything on the side table, spun, and ran out the door.

She stopped, gasping, on the other side.

"Hey, baby! I didn't know you'd be this anxious to see me again!"

Dearborne turned her head to look into the leering face of the police guard. Her initial impulse was to lay into him about letting shadows with swords into the patient's room, but then she managed to collect what was left of her composure. Whatever it was that had sliced and blocked the needles had not yet cut her down, so her best idea was to get out of the hospital fast.

She smoothed her uniform, swallowed, and smiled prettily for the officer. "It gets pretty lonely around here," she told him. "I get off at five."

"I get off at eight," the cop said hopefully.

Dearborne snapped her fingers. "Tough luck," she said and walked away abruptly.

Once she had turned the corner, listening to the cop's cursing and grumbling all the way, she all but ran back to the supply closet. Looking both ways to make sure she wasn't seen, she slipped inside.

Actually, the place was bigger than an average closet. It was only called a closet because it was lined with shelves and windowless. It was a long, tall room, paneled in cedar with a pile of linen on the left set of shelves for the laundry, stacks of neatly folded clean linen on the right, and various surgical aids on the far wall. There was one naked light on the ceiling.

By the back shelves lay Dearborne's bag. Inside was her street clothes: a pair of designer jeans, a French-cut T-shirt, and some high-heeled, open-toed sandals. She was halfway toward them when the same soft voice she had heard in room seven-fifteen spoke again.

"Perfect," it said. "Where do you hide a nurse? Among other nurses."

Claire spun madly around the room, trying to locate the origin of the sound. As she watched, the pile of linen began to grow. Suddenly it was as tall as a man and out of it stepped Brett in the garb of a doctor.

Brett was covered from head to foot in white. A surgical cap covered his hair. A surgical mask covered most of his face. All Claire could see of the unidentified man was his steel-gray eyes.

In his hand was a sack of black. He dropped it to the floor where it spread out. The nurse could see that it was pitch black and blue clothing of some kind. Its color matched that of the darkness.

His arm continued to move up after he had dropped the dark clothing. It stopped when it was perpendicular to his now white-clothed chest. With a flick of his wrist, he spun a three-foot-long scabbard out from behind his arm. He had been holding it so his limb blocked it from view. Claire was speechless as she watched the whole ceremony.

Suddenly, he twirled the sword scabbard in one hand and raised the other so that it gripped the end. With a pull he had dropped the scabbard and was holding a three-foot samurai sword up to the yellow lightbulb's harsh glare. The blade was the same one Dearborne had seen in room seven-fifteen.

"What . . . what are you going to do?" she stammered.

In answer, the sword twirled in his hand until it rested in his palm spear-style, its tip pointed toward the center of Dearborne's chest.

She jumped to the side as soon as he threw it, slamming against the right side shelves as the sword thudded deep into the wood of the rear shelves. She was amazed she was still alive. To prove it to herself, she took one deep breath of relief. As she inhaled, she noticed the perfect straight ten-inch slice in her nursing uniform top. The sword blade had cut the cloth without her knowing it, but not the skin.

She jerked her head in the direction of the white-clad figure. She could not see his mouth, but his eyes were smiling. She looked from the steel-gray orbs to the fingers on his right hand, which were moving. Slipping out of his shirt sleeve and into his hand was a scalpel.

Dearborne felt faint again. There just couldn't be *two* men loose in the hospital who were this dexterous. She realized that this was the same creature who had stopped her in McDonald's room. And somehow, he had left the room, changed clothes, and gotten in the closet before she did.

The knowledge of his ability strengthened the girl. With a feint to the right, she tried to run by him on the left. The scalpel slashed down, blocking her path. She jumped back and looked down in surprise just as the right side of her top flopped open. The man had slashed from the right side of his earlier horizontal cut, straight down vertically to her waist. The perfectly tailored opening revealed the right bra cup.

She pulled her shirt up in vain, for it flopped down again as soon as she leaned back against the right wall shelves. Trying not to telegraph her moves, Claire suddenly leaped toward the rear, wrapping her hands around the hilt of the stuck samurai sword. She gave a mighty tug, expecting the blade to come swinging free so she could cut the man up, but it was stuck good and tight. She looked over her shoulder to see the man slowly approaching. She tugged harder and harder, stepping up on the lower shelves for leverage.

She pulled until she heard the white-garbed man right

behind her. Then she gave one last pull, her teeth gritted and her eyes closed tight with the effort. The sword slipped out of the shelf and swung around, only to sink deeply into the shelf on the other side. Dearborne opened her eyes to see the "doctor" standing four feet away from her, unscathed. Just as her mind began to accept this, the left side of her top dropped open. Now her entire chest was revealed as if she had put on a pair of army long-johns upside down and backwards.

Dearborne crouched, both arms criss-crossing across her chest. She held that position as the man in white took a step forward and reached for her with his right hand. Suddenly Dearborne straightened and drove her right knee as hard as she could between the man's legs. A sound of triumph burst from her lips as she knew she had it timed perfectly. She prepared for the shattering smack of her bone crushing his penis.

The man didn't stop reaching toward her. With seemingly the most casual, but incredibly fast, movement, he swung his left hand over to cup her knee—just millimeters from its target. Kicking his hand was like kicking a five-fingered wall cover in rubber. Her knee simply stopped, none the worse for wear, and dropped back to its original position.

Once Dearborne adjusted to what happened, she saw that the "man" was not reaching for her, but the samurai sword. He held it in his hand, having plucked it out of the shelf as if it were stuck in rice paper. The scalpel was nowhere to be seen. Both his hands wrapped around the sword handle.

The blonde nurse stood hunched and shivering against the rear shelves. Her arms were still crossed across her chest.

"Lower them," said that soft voice.

"Please . . ." she begged, terrified.

"Lower them or lose them," the man advised.

Dearborne dropped her hands to her side, her chin up, only one eye open.

The man stepped forward, sliced down and across in seemingly one smooth motion.

Claire held her breath. She felt no pain, not even the slightest prick or tug. Only when she looked down and exhaled did her bra come off in two pieces. It split open between cups and both strands dropped off. Her round, pointed, cone-like breasts shone in the yellow light. They looked like two cherry-topped mountain peaks stuck to her chest.

She looked at the man who was apparently admiring her figure and his own skill while leaning on the sword like a cane. She opened her mouth to speak and he moved again. The sword spun up into the air and sliced down, seemingly right in front of her nose. She swallowed what she had to say with an audible gulp. As she did, the entire front of her dress opened like an unbuttoned coat.

Then, even more incredibly, her slip broke in half and cascaded to the ground. It was too much for Claire to take.

"Why didn't you try for the panties?" she asked, her voice cracking.

"I didn't want to push your luck," the man flatly replied. His sword was at his side, held loosely in his hand, but Dearborne wasn't fooled. He could manicure her with that thing at ten paces.

"I'm afraid you have me at a disadvantage," she continued, figuring that the ice was broken. "We haven't been properly introduced."

"You're the woman who tried to kill Lynn McDonald,"

102

he immediately answered, his voice cold. "I'm the man who'll find out why."

"No way, honey," Dearborne said with more courage than she felt. "I happen to like living."

"Then you're going to hate dying," Brett said. "As you mentioned, I have you at a disadvantage. You saw what I did with your clothes. Imagine what I could do with your skin." Brett gave her a moment to let it sink in. "You're nothing if not a pragmatist," he continued lightly. "I've got a secret that'll keep you alive. And I'm not about to talk if you cooperate. So you've got a choice. Either trust me or die now."

"What secret?" Dearborne demanded, stalling for time. "You've got nothing on me."

"Bravado," Brett retorted, "the last vestige of a desperate person. You notice I'm not asking you who told you to kill the girl. I'm only asking why."

"Nobody told me!" Claire contended. She was going to say more but the samurai sword's tip was suddenly under her chin. If she opened her mouth now, she'd have a cleft bigger than Kirk Douglas's.

"Keep it quiet," Brett suggested. "It may be four-thirty in the morning and the door might be sound-proofed, but we wouldn't want to take any chances, would we?"

"Nobody told me," Claire hissed between clenched teeth.

With his free hand, Brett held up the doctor's permission form Dearborne hastily left in room seven-fifteen. "As near as I can read doctor's handwriting, this says that Dr. Robert Schenkman gave you permission to go into McDonald's room hiding a syringe. His signature could be faked, but there's one way of finding out. I'll simply ask him."

The expression on Dearborne's face told Brett all he needed to know.

"Now Dr. Schenkman might get very upset if he knew you left a bit of incriminating evidence at the scene of the unsuccessful crime. That would mean she couldn't die without his incriminating himself. And as far as I can tell, he doesn't want her to wake up."

"So you've got all your information," the girl spat. "What do you want from me?"

"Why?" Brett repeated. What he didn't ask was why it was important enough to send seven insane killers to make sure she died.

"I don't know," Claire shrugged indifferently.

The sword flashed again, moving from Brett's side, through the air and back again at incredible speed. A thin red line appeared across her stomach midway between her navel and breasts. This time, she felt it.

"I don't know, I tell you!" she said with conviction. "I just do what I'm told and take the money."

"It's going to hurt next time," Brett warned and then smiled. "It's time to change allegiances, dear."

At that moment, the door to the supply closet swung open. A big black orderly stood in the doorway. Brett's head snapped around. Dearborne collected all the air she could and screamed one loud word.

"Rapel!"

Chapter Five

Brett Wallace stood on the train tracks at five-fifteen in the morning. He felt the locomotive coming before he heard or saw it. The vibrations of its weight came through the metal track on which Brett rested one foot. According to his interior clock, it was only ten minutes late. The Ninja Master smiled. He was not disappointed.

Although he had been taken by surprise back at the hospital—because the supply closet was soundproofed, he couldn't hear outside—and had to throw the charging black man into the shrieking arms of the nearly naked Dearborne, the night was not without its successes. First, there was no way anyone could recognize him with the surgical cap and mask on. Secondly, he knew who was after McDonald. Thirdly, he was sure that the blond nurse would not warn Schenkman that he knew.

No matter who she told her story to, it was her neck on the line—not Schenkman's or his. If she told the doctor about her interrogation, she'd have to admit that she led Brett to the truth. If she told the cops all she knew, Schenkman could say that his signature was faked. Then the guard outside room seven-fifteen would be happy to incriminate who he considered a miserable little cock-teaser. There was no way Dearborne could win unless she kept her mouth shut.

Wallace's only problems were that he was working at a disadvantage and under a time limit. His two confrontations with Lieutenant Anthony forced him to send an alert to Jeff, Rhea, and Hama. If the police did any investigation at all into Brett's background, they'd come up with a blank. That sort of thing would make the police very nervous. So as far as his three associates were concerned, Brett didn't exist until he sounded the "all clear." He wouldn't go near the dojo or the restaurant until the worst of it had blown over.

Thankfully, almost everything he needed was presently on his person. Brett had secured his ninja armament and reversible uniform. On one side was the color of night and on the other the color of daylight. In his sash was his katana, the long sword, and on his back was the wakizashi, the short blade he had terrorized Dearborne with. Around his shoulder was coiled his kyotetsu-shoge, an elastic cord with a two-sided blade on one end and a weight on the other. Along his arm were the poisonous dirks and darts. Around his ankles were his throwing and climbing spikes. Around his waist were the shuriken, the throwing stars which could become little circular saws in the air.

In his hand was a change of clothes. He carried a pair of slacks and a shirt, just in case he had to mingle with the public in daylight. Otherwise he would stay masked and covered, only his eyes showing through his ninja hood. Even the skin around his eyes was darkened, so that if he closed his eyes, he would be all but invisible in the night.

He was prepared to act fast, because he had to. The other problem was that if Dearborne didn't tell Schenkman he was pegged, then the doctor would still consider it open season on Lynn McDonald. Just because the nurse would report that the mission was scrubbed on account of faulty equipment didn't mean the doctor wouldn't try again. And Brett could not be there all the time to ensure the needles broke or were blocked by his own special formula of hardened clay usually reserved for blocking gun barrels.

He had to go to the source of the problem and cure it once and for all. And it wasn't as simple as getting to and killing Schenkman. The doctor might simply be a cog in a larger machine that had sent seven kamikaze psychos and one pragmatic nurse after McDonald. Brett had to find out why it was so important for Lynn to die and eliminate the problem. That was why he was going to Santa Cruz.

Brett had stopped running from the hospital when he reached Lynn's apartment. The police had secured her rooms, but that didn't stop Brett. They had searched her closets, but Brett had stashed his material there after they had left. They had impounded most of her personal things, including her pocketbook, but not before Brett had lifted her clip-on nurse's ID. He had done that right after he blew away the redheaded kid's face.

On it was the name of the establishment Lynn had worked for: the Sanctuary. It had only taken a little checking after that. At the same time Brett announced the alert, he had revved up his NEC computer. It had displayed public records and employment charts showing that Schenkman worked one day a week in the Sausalito hospital while his main job was at the Sanctuary in Santa Cruz. Brett only had to push a few more buttons to find out what the Sanctuary was all about. It was a psychiatric hospital for the criminally insane.

If the police had discovered the ID, they would have asked a lot of questions, thereby warning Schenkman of impending danger so he could cover his tracks. And even if they traced McDonald's attackers to the madhouse, they'd be hard presed to pin anything on Schenkman. There would be no way to prove that anyone ordered the crazies to kill. The simplest excuse would be that a bunch of them escaped and went after the nurse of their own volition. Even if the case got to the court, the lawyers would have a field day.

Meanwhile McDonald could stay in her coma and never wake up, or slip into death "by natural causes." Nurse Dearborne showed how easily that could be arranged if Brett wasn't around. As Brett thought about it, the freight train moving south along the California coast pulled into sight. Brett could see it, but the engineer couldn't see him. The Ninja Master stood on a straightaway between two curves. The locomotive would have to slow to make the turns.

Brett merely stepped to the side of the tracks and allowed the engine to pass him at the distance of a half foot. He allowed half the cars of the train to go by before he crouched. Even though the thing had slowed, the wheels were hurtling by at a furious pace. There was hardly a second's time between wheels as they passed Brett. He shoved his street clothes into his sash and shifted his weight to the balls of his feet. Just as the rear wheel of one car passed, he dove forward, pulling his body sideways in midair. He leaped between the front and rear wheels of the following car, grabbed the undercarriage and pulled his body up. He was now tightly stuck to the bottom of the car, riding the rails like a leech.

Brett dug his feet and hands deeper into the undercarriage. If the train continued on schedule, it would take ninety minutes to reach the outskirts of Santa Cruz. Wallace settled in for the ride. If, for some reason,

Sausalito's Lieutenant Anthony got bored investigating the Hansen murders and decided to stake out Brett's car, he'd have a long wait.

Dawn broke over the Sanctuary. The deep red, purple and yellow sky set off the gray, squat outlines of the structure. It was a combination of steel and concrete boxes, its large windows covered with chain-link metal screens. It lay nestled in the sumptuous green and brown of the Santa Cruz hills, interrupting the evergreen woodland around it like a festering sore.

There was one large, main metal gate, which opened sideways. There were rollers on the bottom and a pulley system near the top. Above the pulley stretched three strands of barbed wire. The barbed wire continued along the top of the fifteen-foot-high fence all the way around, held in place by rods set at forty-five-degree angles from the top of the links.

Ten feet away from the first fence was another one exactly like it, only its rolling gate moved in the opposite direction from the first. There was a guard's shack in front of the first fence—for people coming in—and one in back of the second fence—for people leaving. There was one guard in each shack and each man wore a .38 caliber revolver in a hip holster. On the uniform cap and on the shoulder was a patch depicting two open hands holding a bright, rising sun—the Sanctuary symbol.

Brett was not unduly impressed or surprised by the lack of visible guards. Once an "alleged perpetrator" was found "unfit to stand trial," he was thrown to the doctors and—if the truth be known—neither the legal establishment nor the law enforcement agencies want to see the accused again. The rest of humanity wasn't too thrilled over the prospect of meeting these society rejects either.

So when a psychiatric institute was created in or near a town, it produced the same sort of response as the bubonic plague.

Since no one wanted to visit, and no one wanted anyone inside to leave, the government which funded these places managed to cut costs by maintaining only a skeleton security staff. Brett considered all this as he marched right up to the main gate and the guard posted there. All the security guard saw was an innocuous man, about five-foot-eleven, with sandy—almost brown—hair and light eyes, wearing a white shirt with dark slacks.

"Can I help you?" he asked.

"Yes," said Brett calmly. "I'd like to see Dr. Schenkman. Tell him it's about Lynn McDonald."

Wallace did not have to wait long. The guard made a quick call on the black, old-fashioned, heavy phone inside the shack—which Brett noticed had no dial, but a single button instead—and the two tall chain-link fence gates rolled back to the sound of a bell ringing. The second guard, a wizened old man, walked him to the main entrance where a chubby, cherubic man sporting a crew cut was waiting.

"Mister . . . ?" he asked, extending a porcine hand.

"Wallace," Brett answered, figuring it didn't pay to use a new fake name, since McDonald, Anthony, and no doubt Dearborne knew him as Wallace.

"Hello, Mr. Wallace," said the cherubic man in a suit and lab coat. "I'm Dr. Parker, Dr. Schenkman's right-hand man. I'll take you to him. Please don't be tense and try to ignore anything unusual."

The two walked through tall, wide, sunlit hallways—most of them lined with mesh-covered windows—and passed various patients ranging from well-dressed, confused-looking men to robed, gibbering wrecks.

"Is it safe to have them all out like this?" Brett inquired.

"Oh, them?" Parker exclaimed, as if he hadn't noticed the people as they walked by. "They're perfectly harmless. The dangerous ones are kept in another wing completely."

As if on cue, they rounded a corner and came to a hallway sealed at one end by a metal door equipped with a small, sliding panel. Parker knocked. The panel slipped open. Another harmless-looking security guard peered out.

"Oh, Dr. Parker," he said. "It's you."

"Yes, it's me," the man said pleasantly, a smile stuck to his face. "Open up, will you?"

Brett heard a bolt slide back and then the metal door creaked open. Both men entered a hallway almost exactly like the first, except the windows were not covered in chain-link mesh. The hallway ended with a single door. Parker brought Brett right up to it.

"Dr. Schenkman should be in," he said. "Please knock and then go right in." With that, Parker turned and walked back the way he had come, smiling into all the rooms as he passed.

Brett watched his progress and then turned to the door. Placing one hand on the plain doorknob, he knocked with the knuckle of his first finger. Almost immediately, he turned the knob and pushed the obstruction out of his way. The door swung open to reveal a wide, comfortable office. The floor was carpeted in beige pile, the walls were lined with oak bookshelves, and there was a wide wooden desk at the rear wall in front of a large, reinforced, alarm-lined picture window. The clear glass looked out upon the Sanctuary's back yard, its set of fence enclosures, and the beautiful woodlands beyond.

Seated behind the desk, busying himself with some paperwork, was a black-haired man with a strong, angular face.

"Dr. Schenkman?" Brett asked.

The man looked up, his blue eyes dark and clear in the morning light. He rose, showing himself to be at least six-feet-four. He wore pinstriped trousers and vest and had his shirt seeves rolled up. Both his suit coat and a lab jacket were on the hooks of a standing wooden rack next to the desk.

"Mr. Wallace?" he asked back, putting his hand out. Brett nodded as he shook the man's large, bony palm. "Please sit down," he invited, motioning to a single chair to the right of his desk. Brett complied. "Now," said Schenkman. "What can I do for you?" He put his hands on the desk and stared at Wallace.

"It's about Lynn McDonald," Brett said uncomfortably.

"Lynn McDonald?" Schenkman repeated, not taking his dark blue eyes off the bridge of Brett's nose. "Who's that?"

Brett said nothing, his face blank.

"One of my patients?" Schenkman said abruptly, as if he hadn't expected Brett to answer. He then paused, saying nothing more until Brett replied eleven seconds later.

"One of your nurses," he said slowly.

"Oh?" Schenkman retorted. "Which one?"

The doctor hadn't changed his position or manner during the entire conversation. His eyes bore through Brett and he talked like a drowning man—gulping in air and pushing it out into harsh-sounding words.

Brett felt the incongruity of describing the girl in the office, but he did it anyway. "About five-seven, slim, auburn hair. . . ."

"Oh, yes, oh yes, oh yes," Schenkman interrupted, leaning back and laying his palms flat on the desk. "I remember now." He returned to rivet Brett with his stare. "What about her?"

Brett paused, not completely believing the situation. He was expecting a careful, guilty man who'd handle him with kid gloves. What he got was a man who seemingly couldn't be less concerned and acted as if he wouldn't give Brett the time of day unless pushed. Brett decided to push a little.

"She's in a coma in a Sausalito hospital," Brett answered, a tinge of impatience in his voice.

"I'm sorry to hear that," Schenkman snapped back. "So?"

"So?" Brett responded incredulously.

"Mr. Wallace," Schenkman intoned, rising from his desk by putting his big hands down on the blotter and pushing. "I am running a psychiatric hospital. I am trying to cure people the state has labeled as criminally dangerous. I don't have time to keep up with the private lives of my nurses. If you have anything to say to me, please say it. Otherwise please take it up with Dr. Parker and the personnel office." Schenkman wound up standing with his back to the window, the light creating an eerie glow around him.

Brett was unfazed. The doctor had told him a few things he needed to know. First, that Schenkman himself was the boss. Second, that he would be interested to know how much Brett knew. Brett decided to tell him. He sat in the chair, crossed his legs and grinned. "She told me to come see you if anything happened to her," he lied.

The information didn't fluster Schenkman. He did not move. "What are you to her?" he asked.

Score one for the good guys, Brett thought. Schenkman was beginning to dig, rather than just respond. "A friend," Brett drawled knowingly. "A very *good* friend."

"Why would she tell you to see me?" he said innocently.

"For money," Brett answered, looking at the back of his hands. "Isn't it funny, doctor, that she was attacked by two separate groups of people before she was injured? And that these people would be willing to kill themselves rather than be captured? Sounds like pretty criminally dangerous people, doesn't it?"

"My patients are persecuted individuals, Mr. Wallace!" Schenkman flared. "They made single mistakes in their sorry lives. I'm trying to cure them of their psychoses, and you have the gall to come in here and suggest—"

"You want me to talk to the cops about it?" Brett interrupted. That quieted Schenkman down immediately.

"What do you mean?" he asked, leaning over his desk. "It is the police who seek to persecute my patients."

"Can the rhetoric," Brett suggested. "They might be interested to know where Lynn worked before she was attacked. She told them she was a temporary with a nursing service, and I lifted her Sanctuary ID before the cops could see it. They might like to see it now, unless you're a little more cooperative."

Schenkman remained perfectly still and perfectly quiet in front of the window for a half a minute. Then he pulled out the pen from his desk set and leaned over a memo pad. "Where are you staying?" he asked flatly.

"In town," said Brett.

"Go to this address at one o'clock this evening," Schenkman suggested, scribbling down an address on the pad and handing the page to Brett. "I'm sure we can come to some sort of arrangement."

Brett smiled smugly and took the proffered paper. He folded and put it in his pocket without looking at it. There was plenty of time for that. "That's more like it," he said. "One o'clock tonight. It's a date." Brett suddenly realized that was the last thing he said to Lynn. He rose from the chair as Schenkman turned his back on him and stared out the window.

"Can you find your way out?" he asked without looking back.

"Sure," said Brett easily. He turned and walked toward the door just as a small knock came from the other side. He had his hand on the knob just as someone outside twisted and pushed in. The door swung in and Brett was standing face to face with Nurse Claire Dearborne.

Brett managed to hold onto his supercilious expression, while the girl's eyes widened and jaw dropped. Her lips bounced off each other twice before Schenkman interrupted her confusion. "Yes, nurse, what is it?" he asked curtly.

Dearborne looked to the doctor, then back at Brett, then back to the doctor. Finally she was able to compose herself. "Dr. Swartz wanted you to see this," she said, holding up a file.

"Well, come in, come in," Schenkman said impatiently. Then he added pointedly, "And close the door after you."

Dearborne took one last veiled—almost shy—look at Brett before she did what she was told. The thick door shut in Brett's face as he left, but not before he heard the beginning of their conversation.

"Do you know who that is?" the girl asked. "That's the guy who was with McDonald when they brought her in."

"I know," was what Schenkman replied.

Brett held his smile until he reached the end of the administration wing. He noted, as he walked, that every office door was shut and every window in the doors was made of opaque glass. He remembered that all the doors had been closed on the way in, except for two that were empty of people. And he remembered Dr. Parker's smiling, nodding head as he walked out. No doubt work in a place like this affected a man after awhile. Brett just didn't like the way it seemed to be affecting them.

The smile disappeared as he nodded to the guard, who let him out. The door closed behind him and he was left in the hall of supposedly harmless mental cases. Brett walked straight down the center of the wide floor, thinking about what he had accomplished. As far as he knew his visit was a success. He had alerted Schenkman that someone suspected that something was very wrong. He had done it without endangering Dearborne, who may not have connected her strip-interrogator in the closet with the innocent looking boyfriend of Nurse McDonald.

Now Schenkman couldn't kill McDonald without getting him out of the way first. Brett was far more dangerous to him in his condition than Lynn was in hers. Wallace could rest assured that Lynn would rest peacefully in San Francisco while he took the heat in Santa Cruz.

"Have a nut then?" screeched a high-pitched voice into his face. "Isn't that a pretty dolly? Aren't the girls good, then?" One man had ran out of his room to yell at Brett as he passed by. Brett kept moving, not turning his head, while his eyes looked for some doctor, nurse, or aide. But he did not see or hear anyone coming.

"Have a sweet?" the man cried. "Yes or no? A sweet or a nut, either is fine. Yes or no?" he continued, keeping up with Brett's stride and yelling at his profile. Others laughed and gibbered in support as the duo walked past.

"No," said Brett. He kept moving, but the accosting man stopped immediately.

"Aw," he complained to the floor. "So good, too. So good. Really." He looked after Brett, suddenly angry. "Have a sweet," he screamed, shaking.

Brett marveled at the lack of care and consideration provided by places like this. First, the death penalty is abolished so asylums are filled to overflowing, and then they cut back funds, thinking the killers aren't worth it, so not enough people are hired to control them. And even when there is enough money, most of the menial shepherding jobs go to sadists. Almost everybody else would rather be an undertaker than an asylum attendant.

Another guard opened the front door for him. He made the long walk to the fence without incident. The two gates spread open as the bell rang.

"Have a nice day," said the wizened old guard on the inside.

Brett dug up his material from where he had buried it in the woods and walked into town. The address Schenkman had given him was for a motel. Thinking there was nothing better to do, Brett checked in, managing to get a room adjacent to the one the doctor had noted. He noticed that the room in question was already reserved. Probably permanently reserved by Schenkman, Brett thought. For what reason, he didn't know yet.

The rest of the day he spent in the library and on the streets in the immediate vicinity of the motel. By the time he returned to his room, he knew every single nook, cranny, and turn in the area. He had plotted the best ways in and out of the hills as well as the center of town.

After a fresh seafood dinner at Santa Cruz's version of San Francisco's Fisherman's Wharf, Brett returned to the motel and broke into the next room through its locked double doors. By all evidence it was a classically dull motel room. The door was near the back of the room, on the right-hand wall. To the right of the door was a little nook with a writing table moored to the wall. To the table's left was the bathroom, tiled in white and with a tub between sink and toilet.

To the left of the door was a double bed. Across from that stood a bureau with a mirror, and next to it was a television on a rolling stand. On the left-hand wall next to the bed was the front door, which led outside, and a picture window which was shuttered by a closed venetian blind. Brett made a circuit of the room, knelt down by the bed, adjusted its metal frame, made a few more changes to suit him, then went back into his own room to wait.

One o'clock found Brett cross-legged on his bed, meditating. He sought that level of inner peace which could make him remorselessly deadly. Once he reached that point, he would see other people's movements as if they were in slow motion. Once he rose to that level, his mind and body would be perfectly in tune, and his limbs would seem to move without conscious effort.

In the meantime, his consciousness centered on more earthly matters. Utilizing what information he had before, plus what he collected at the library, he put together a monstrous, but feasible plot. Schenkman had sent murderers after McDonald because she knew too much. But when she met Brett, she did not act like anyone who knew a deadly secret. Obviously, she wasn't aware that she knew Schenkman's secret.

Brett's mind drifted back to his meetings with Lieutenant Anthony. He remembered the police officer saying that he was late for a meeting with the Marin County cops to compare notes on the Hansen and Beymer killings. He remembered his own thought that the attacks on Lynn matched the insanity and ferocity of the family massacres. The only difference was that the Hansen and

Beymer victims didn't have a Ninja Master to protect them.

Assuming there was a connection, the big question was why McDonald had to die and why the Hansens and Beymers had to die. The library cleared up part of that problem. Utilizing the microfilm viewer, Brett had established a connection between the two families. Both Mr. Hansen and Mr. Beymer worked for the same corporation under the aegis of two different companies. Even if the police found this connection, it wouldn't surprise them. TransTotal West, the company in question, owns hundreds of businesses across the country. It was a coincidence, but not an unlikely one, that the fathers of two ravaged households would work, unknowingly, for the same corporation. And their deaths certainly did not seem to be professional "hits." Not when all the children and wives were so viciously butchered.

The last piece Brett had in his puzzle was that the headquarters for TransTotal West was in Santa Cruz. Really not very far from the Sanctuary—as the crow flies. Somehow Schenkman had made a deal with someone high up at TransTotal. Somehow, without knowing it, Lynn had gotten wind of it. And somehow Brett had to get to the bottom of it.

He remembered the piles of gore and pools of blood that had not dried at the Hansen house, even the next day. He remembered the laughing, burning faces of the diner attacker, the old woman, and the redheaded kid. He remembered the look of fear, sadness, and guilt on Lynn's face. He remembered to full consciousness, wanting revenge, needing it. Then he heard someone enter the next room.

He wore his black top and black stretch slacks. He

put the rest of his material under the bed. Then he walked to the double door. He had left his side open and the other side unlocked. All he had to do was turn the knob and push in. The first noise of his entrance came when the door swung back and hit the writing desk's chair.

Brett was leaning nonchalantly against the doorframe when the blond on the bed gasped and whirled around. Claire Dearborne had been sitting on the left edge of the bed, intent on the front door. Her eyes were wide and shocked when she turned around. As soon as she saw it was Brett, she breathed a quick sigh of relief and jumped off the bed, running into his arms.

The girl wrapped herself around him, her head on his chest. "Oh, thank God!" she said, her voice muffled. "Thank God you're all right."

Brett took her by the elbows and pulled her away from him. "Didn't you think I would be?" he asked smugly, his con-man persona in place.

"You don't know Schenkman," she breathed in hushed tones. "I didn't know what he'd do. It was all I could do to convince him to let me meet you instead of his hired thugs."

Brett closed the door after him, and walked past her into the room. "Well, now that you are here, did you bring the money?" He turned back when she didn't reply. She was wearing a raincoat, a scarf, and Frye boots.

"Well, he didn't say anything about money," she said coyly, moving over to the edge of the bed. "He just said I should come and talk about price." As she was talking, she undid the coat's belt and buttons. When she let it fall open, Brett could see she had nearly nothing on underneath.

Nearly nothing included her Frye boots, with kneesocks folded down to mid-calf, a lacy burgundy-colored teddi, and a single strand of gold around her neck. "Will I do as down payment?" she said shamelessly.

No, Brett thought, she hadn't made the connection between the innocuous looking boyfriend and the steel-eyed swordsman in the supply closet. Either that, or she was one hell of an nymphomaniacal actress. "Well," he said with a smile. "There's no reason we can't *talk* about it."

He moved over and put one arm around her. She pulled him down to a sitting position on the bed. She started on his lips, her hands massaging his head, and then worked her way around. Her eyes were closed; not in lust, Brett saw—his eyes were open—but in concentration. She was working very hard to seduce him and she was doing a very wet job of it. Brett saw no reason not to go along, but he also saw no reason not to make it just a little difficult. It would build her character, he reasoned.

Brett kissed back, but he made it seem as if he were surprised at the passion of her attack. For a few seconds, he just didn't seem to know where to put his hands. Claire kept kissing and breathing heavily, making little gasping noises between puckers. Finally, raising her eyebrows in consternation, she grabbed his hand and laid it over her breast. When he didn't do anything, she opened her eyes in perplexity. His eyes were closed, seemingly caught up in the ardor. When she closed her eyes again, his opened.

Next, she tried to move his hand on her breast in a circular motion. Like a stubborn lawnmower which finally turns on with the hundredth tug of its cord, Brett continued the tit-grind under his own power. Her hand free, Claire began to tear at his shirt and belt buckle. He reached down to assist, only to have his hand forcefully

121

returned to her firm chest. Unbeknown to Dearborne, however, he had undone his belt, just to make sure she didn't stumble onto the four-bladed shuriken in its buckle holder.

Dearborne pulled Brett on top of her as she fell backward onto the bed. Her lips left his and began assailing his neck and ear. In between licks she would gasp instructions. "My nightie . . . clasps . . . at top . . . between legs . . . do it . . . oh, please do it!"

Brett's head was sunk deep into her blond hair next to her ear. He smiled, widely, with the first real pleasure he felt in days. He'd do it, all right. She asked for it.

His mouth began to work on her neck.

"The clasps," she began again, and then stopped, speechless. She had felt something. It was a distant, tiny feeling, but it was there. It was not something she felt on top of her skin. It was not something she felt between her legs. It was actually something she felt inside her. And it felt good.

Her head jerked slightly to the side. There it was again, stronger this time. An honest-to-God feeling. Something that clouded her mind and caressed her brain. She felt like giggling in complete, carefree pleasure. But before she could get used to it, it happened again. Ignoring the conscious part of her brain completely, she found her body shuddering with delight.

"No," the last remaining rational part said aloud, her hands trying to guide him toward her crotch. "The snaps . . . I mean the clasps!" This time she did giggle— happily, girlishly. She hadn't felt like this in twenty years.

Without pausing, Brett gently knocked her hands away. They fell softly to the bed on either side of her head. He kept working on her pressure points on and about the skull as she luxuriated in it. Her legs were moving slowly back and forth, rubbing against each other, while her mouth was shaped in a sensual "O," making cooing noises.

As he kissed, bit and licked, Brett's hands then slid down to her sternum. Wtih a quick motion, the top clasps sprung open and he slipped the silk down to reveal her sprightly breasts. His hand replaced his lips at her neck. His mouth went to work down below.

By the fifth minute of his assault, Claire couldn't remember her name. By the sixth. she was helpless. She was floating on a cloud of her own joy, feeling sensations she had never felt before. By the time Brett got down to her clitoris, her lubrication had made a puddle on the bed covers.

She couldn't speak. All she could do was pray to herself. "Please do it. Oh God, please make him do it. I want it so badly. Oh God, please!" She wasn't even aware Brett had undone the snaps down there as well. He entered her with his hand first, letting his other hand continue on her torso. He worked her up just to the point of a cataclysmic orgasm and then abruptly stopped.

Claire rose from her lying position like an intercontinental ballistic missile. Her mouth was open, but all that came out was a squawk of frustration. In that second, Brett grabbed the bed covers under her and pulled like a magician who pulls a tablecloth from under a banquet without disturbing a thing. The covers whipped out from under Dearborne. Brett instantly snapped it back, so it floated down across Claire's body. When she saw that his pants were off, his penis was stiff, and he was returning, she laid back on the pillows and sighed.

But one part of her mind had snapped out of the spell. That part of her mind began to make comparisons. That part of her mind suddenly remembered where she had seen that kind of style and skill before.

"You!" she cried as he slid his throbbing key into her creamy lock.

Her head rose up so that his waiting hand went right over her lips. "You finally got it," he said, his voice becoming the whisper she had heard in the supply closet and room seven-fifteen. But even as he said it, his body was moving imperceptibly. She wanted to say more, but the sensations held her captive again. She drifted back upon the pillows, her body engulfed in rapture.

Once again, he carried her to the very apex of her senses. But just before she reached the summit, the door of the motel room burst in.

Coming right behind the door were two men in uniform holding guns. The bliss turned off inside her as if it had been controlled by a light switch.

"No!" she shouted, unable to contain herself. But Brett was already out of her and on his back, facing the pointed revolvers of the men in the Sanctuary security uniforms.

"Having a sweet, eh?" said the first man. Brett had expected something like this to happen, and he heard the men approaching outside, but he was honestly taken aback by the appearance of the first man. Even though he was wearing the security uniform and the hat was pulled tightly on his head, the first man was unmistakably the psycho who had accosted him in the hallway.

"We caught you red-handed raping this girl, mister," the first man continued quickly. "She'll testify to that." He looked irritably at the girl, who hadn't moved since their entrance. "Get the hell out of the way, missy," he whined. She suddenly jumped up, as if Brett were a centipede lying next to her. She hastily tried to snap her nightie back together.

"Well sir," the first man went on. "You raped her and resisted arrest, so we had to kill you." He turned to the other guard next to him. "We'll say he was a nut who escaped from the Sanctuary and kidnapped her, huh?"

The other man chuckled. "Yeah," he agreed. "A dangerous psychotic. We had no choice but to shoot him on sight." The man waited for Brett to react. But the sandy-haired man in the bed sat still, only reacting internally to the fact that the second man was the wizened guard who had been in the second shack.

When Brett said nothing, the wizened man continued. "So you're the hero, huh? Great, big hero, right? Come charging into that place. Push the kid into the laundry room and shoot him six times, didn't you? Watched the woman fry, did you?" Brett remained motionless and silent, his face a cautious, intent mask.

"Well, those two were my wife and son!" the wizened man seethed. "You killed my boy!" he cried, the gun shaking as he moved forward.

Brett saw the muscle tense, the vein appear, and the skin move. The wizened man was pulling the trigger to relieve his anguish.

The bedspread puffed up as if a ball of air had popped underneath. The .38 bullet dug right into the mattress where Brett's chest had been. At the same moment the pistol bucked in the old man's hand, the wakizashi blade chopped his face in two.

Brett had adjusted the bed frame earlier so that there was a space between the box spring and the metal holder. In the sheath-like space, he had placed the naked samurai blade. With his right hand he had pulled it up, sliced the sheet away as if it weren't there, and cut a three-inch-deep gash in the old man's face from his chin to his brow.

Blood gushed from the opening like tomato juice pouring from a can. The man's hands went up on either side of his face, but he couldn't get them to reach the wound. They vibrated next to his ears, he choked on the crimson liquid pouring into his mouth, and fell forward, twitching.

It happened so fast that the first man was still pointing his gun at the bed. He was only able to turn his head before Brett brought the sword down across his neck. The man saw Wallace standing naked on the bed at the same instant blood sprayed out of his throat like the foam on a cresting ocean wave. He saw the spume fall from the corner of his eye and then he fell after it.

Claire Dearborne witnessed it all from the side of the bed. She felt the air from the open door on her back and spun to run out of the room. But when she turned, the door was closed, and there was a samurai blade stuck near the top of it. She spun back toward the bed. She was nose to nose with Brett Wallace.

"I told you it was time to change sides," he said with deadly seriousness. "You didn't listen."

"I didn't know those men were coming," she pleaded, tears welling up. "I swear!"

The sword came out of the door. He grabbed her wrist and threw her onto the bed. She actually sailed across the room without touching the floor and bounced on the bloody mattress. He seemed to have expended no more strength than a man throwing a Frisbee.

"The time for lies is through," he said, coming toward her.

"What are you going to do?" she whispered. Suddenly

she was sure that he could cause her as much pain as he had given her pleasure.

The sword spun in his hand again and sunk deep into the mattress between her legs. "I'm going to let you tell me everything I need to know," he said flatly.

Chapter Six

The murder teams all went out at the same time, Brett learned. That's why the Hansens, the Beymers, and their friends died at about the same time McDonald was attacked. Claire, who actually was a nurse, was placed in the San Francisco hospital where Lynn was working as a temp after her stint at the Sanctuary. That's why the blond was already there when they brought the comatose body of McDonald in. The one thing Dearborne couldn't tell Brett was what McDonald had seen or heard which made her so dangerous.

Brett believed her. His ninja teachers had trained him to be a living lie detector. He believed her when she said that the only reason she had kept quiet about the murders was because she wasn't directly involved and the money was too good. Only when she was called on to kill Lynn herself and keep Brett busy did she begin to see the error of her ways. Up until that point, however, she was just happy to be on the profitable payroll.

The money was coming from one Franklin Delia, president of TransTotal West. Claire only knew that Delia wanted the heads of two of his lesser companies out of the way and paid extremely handsome sums for the service.

So Brett was still in the dark as to the exact reason why Lynn McDonald had to die, but at least he had a reason for being in the dark on this particular Santa Cruz night.

Schenkman was closing the circle. At the same time he had dispatched the wizened man and the sweets man to back up Claire, he had sent out the trio who killed the Hansens and the Beymers to settle accounts with Delia. The TransTotal boss would be in his building late that night, waiting with the final payoff. The three men would collect it, then make sure there was no witness left who could identify them or their leader. In other words, Delia would pay for his crimes. The hard way.

Brett let Claire go. Since she hadn't blown his cover yet, he was doubly certain she would not betray him now. In fact, he reasoned, it was better to have her back at the Sanctuary. First, she might allay Schenkman's suspicions when the wizened and sweets man failed to return; and second, it was good to have someone on the inside when the time came to settle accounts.

Brett moved silently toward the main entrance of the TransTotal West building. It was a tower of black glass and steel beams, standing out like a cemetery headstone in the cloudy night. As the wispy strands of mist passed by the moon, they blocked out the dark silhouette of the Ninja Master as he moved. Everything was in place on his traditional uniform as he reached the door. He was covered head to foot in black, and the black was covered with his sharp, poisoned weapons.

The doors were locked—bolted by a thick piece of metal stretching from one door to the next. Brett's wakizashi seemed to leap out of the scabbard on his back into his open hand as he held it above his shoulder. He then merely inserted the thin blade between the doors and cut down on the steel block. The Japanese sword, made in its secret, ancient way, was far too strong for the bolt. It fell away, sliced into two neat pieces. Brett pushed the door open with his leg.

Something annoyed him as he moved across the grandly appointed lobby toward the bank of escalators, elevators, and service doors. There was something about the motel confrontation which disturbed him deeply. Brett hastily eliminated the thought from his mind. He couldn't afford to concentrate on anything but the two kinds of killers upstairs. There would be the maniacs in front of the desk—the men paid to satisfy their perverted blood-lusts. And there would be the man behind the desk—the one who casually eradicated others in the sacred name of "business." Brett wasn't sure who was worse.

A second later, he stopped thinking about moral judgments. There was no worse or better in this situation. He remembered what his teacher had said. "One does not see something as evil. Evil is. One knows evil, one does not have to 'see' it." Brett knew evil existed in that building, that night. And he vowed that in the next few minutes, either he—or the evil—would be destroyed.

The three men marched along the seventh floor hallway, the night lights casting gloomy shadows on the beige walls as they passed. They were wearing baseball jackets, slacks, shirts, and sneakers. Inside their jackets each man had a .357 revolver and a hunting knife.

"There's nothing we can do this time," the greasy-haired one complained. "All the movies we see have girls dying. There are no girls in here."

"Idiot," said the other one, with thinning brown hair. "Don't you remember 'Schizoid'? There was a big gun fight in a skyscraper just like this one. The guy finally got killed with a letter opener or a stapler or something."

"Naw," said the third man, the big, fat one. "He got shot with his own gun. During a struggle or fight or something."

"Anyway," said the second man. "It was in a skyscraper just like this one."

"Yeah?" said the greasy-haired man, with renewed interest.

"Yeah," said the man with brown hair, with casual assurance.

"Well, that's all right, then," said the greasy-haired man.

The three rounded a corner, becoming excited about the meeting. They stopped at a Plexiglas double door at the end of the hall. On it was stenciled; "Office of Franklin W. Delia, President." The greasy-haired man looked at the man with brown hair with an eager smile. The fat man put one hand inside his jacket pocket and pushed the swinging door open with the other. The trio crossed an empty outer office to a red plush paneled door behind a secretary's desk. As they neared it, an electronic snap could be heard and the door's lock released. Delia was waiting for them.

The fat man looked around the office. There were video cameras in all four corners. There were probably cameras all over the building. Delia had watched their every move from the moment they got on the elevator. The fat man snorted. A lot of good it was going to do him, he figured.

The fat man looked back at the red plush door and pushed it all the way in.

The three killers entered a black glass cell. It was a big, handsomely appointed cell, but a cell nevertheless. The rear wall was shaped like a bay window, with one-way glass covering most of it. Delia could look out, but no one could look in. His desk was right in front of the three-paned window, giving the impression that he was floating above the city. To either side of his desk stood two burly men—four in all. They stood, holding their hands in front of their crotches, their heads nearly cocked to the side.

The three killers stood in a line before the desk. "We came for the money," said the fat man.

Delia was as well groomed and decked out as his money could make him. His black, curly hair had been straightened, and layered over his wisps of gray. The premature age spots had been creamed over. The broken bones in the nose had been replaced with plastic. The body received just as much exercise as it needed to keep his belly from hanging over his belt. He was clad in a perfectly tailored, tasteful three-piece suit. But his black-pupiled eyes were cold and unchanged since youth.

He lifted a small package, wrapped and ribboned like a box of Godiva chocolates. "Here it is," he said, and tosssed it to the edge of the desk.

The fat man scooped it up without ceremony and tore off the delicate wrappings. He lifted the top and flipped through the cash. "It's not enough," he said, passing judgment.

Delia leaned back in his seat, silent. He took a moment to survey the row of eight tiny black and white screens installed just under the lip of his desk. The building was empty of everything, except for shadows.

"What do you mean?" he asked, his black eyes rising to look into the fat man's.

"Just what I said," the fat man replied, his two friends beginning to ease slowly away from him. They kept their movements nonchalant, but they were obvious, nevertheless. "It's not enough," the fat man continued. "We figured this pay for the two men, but we left a lot more dead people behind. We figure you should pay for them too."

"I did not order their deaths," Delia said softly.

The fat man shrugged and said, "Unavoidable. We also figure you should pay for our silence. We know who pointed the finger and you'll never be able to get rid of all of us. So you'll just have to drop off some each month."

Delia started to laugh. It started as a small chuckle, but rose in volume and mirth. Finally he leaned forward, wiping his eyes. "I knew this would happen," he said agreeably. "I knew this would happen as soon as I found out you weren't professional." Just as suddenly as he laughed, Delia became serious, a finger pointed at the fat man. "Well, let me tell you something. I can destroy you a lot easier than you can hurt me. I'm the head of a major corporation. I have respect. Who's going to believe your word against mine?" He started laughing again. "Who's going to believe you at all?"

The fat man smiled along with Delia. Schenkman had told him that this would happen. They plotted the whole thing so that Delia's men would be taken by surprise. The fat man nodded at Delia's assessment of the situation, then spoke quickly and quietly. "Then we'll just have to kill you."

Everyone moved at once, but no one was faster than Brett Wallace. The air-conditioning duct on the wall snapped from its frame. It hardly seemed large enough to hold a dog, but somehow Brett flowed out of it like a liquid man. His arm was in the air first, followed by his head. There was a cracking noise as his shoulder slid into the open at a seemingly impossible angle from his head. Then his second arm was out and the rest of his body followed easily.

He dove out into the office, flipped in the air, and landed feet first in the middle of Delia's desk.

Brett took charge the moment his entrance surprised the madmen. Their target was suddenly blocked. Even though their guns were out, they paused a second in shock. Suddenly both swords were in Brett's hands. The wakizashi blade shone in the dim office light while the katana was still in its scabbard. Brett pushed the unsheathed tip against Delia's chest, toppling the man over backward into his chair, while he cut a vertical slice in the thick desk top. He jumped and smashed down on the cut just as the three killers fired.

Brett went right through the desk to the floor. The bullets shot over his head and passed Delia's prone face to smash into the window. The black glass didn't shatter, but suddenly its center was marred by a network of spider-webbed cracks. The short sword was on the carpet at Brett's feet. He put both hands on either side of the hole he had made in the desk top, lifted, and pushed.

The huge desk leaped off the floor and smashed into the three killers. The brown-haired man's wrist was broken as the heavy desk hit the gun and bent his hand back. The greasy-haired man was thrown back out into the waiting room by the blow. The fat man was knocked to the ground, his gun bouncing away from him. Without looking back, all three men scrambled out of the office. It was the first time things had gone wrong and they were brave only with helpless teenagers and ignorant victims.

Brett stood in the middle of Delia's four bodyguards,

whose hands were moving toward their shoulder-holstered guns while moving in on him. He moved incredibly fast. With one foot, he moved the wakizashi off the floor.

It looked as if he had merely stamped his black-garbed foot and the sword floated up to his hand. But instead of catching it, Brett swung his left hand at the end of its handle while pulling a spike from its holder on his up-raised right ankle with his right hand. The wakizashi was propelled into the stomach of the first guard just as Brett swung the spike up at the second guard whose hand was wrapped around his gun butt.

That was as far as the second guard got. The spike went through his jacket, through his hand, and into his chest. The nail-like spear only stopped when its cap hit the coat cloth. It looked like someone had hammered the spike into him. His jacket was attached to his hand which was attached to his chest. The man whimpered in stunned pain and stumbled back, his pierced arm barely quivering. The first guard fell forward, his hands wrapped around the sword in his stomach, his palms gushing blood as he tried to pull the razor-sharp blade out.

Brett had already killed the other two guards by the time the first two dropped. Even as he was throwing the spike and the wakizashi, he was pivoting his body. The third guard made the mistake of moving in too close. Brett's right foot lashed out, smashing him in the chest. The man flew backward into the cracked window. His weight was too much for the weakened window to bear. It shattered around him, and he fell seven stories in a backward swan dive.

The last guard got his gun out of its holster and aimed it. He was just about to pull the trigger when Brett's body blurred and then took shape crouched before him. The guard saw that Brett's long blade was out and held all the way to the right. At first, the guard thought the man in black hadn't swung the sword yet. But then he remembered seeing a flash of steel. Suddenly he became aware of a wetness on his chin. His free hand rose and touched his jaw. It came away red. But it wasn't a very deep cut, he thought. Hardly more than a scratch. He wondered why it was so hard to pull the gun's trigger. The fourth guard fell over dead from the poison coated blade just as he finished that last thought.

Brett rose and retrieved the short sword from the body of the second guard. His blood had washed off almost all the poison. And until Brett slipped it back in its scabbard, it wouldn't be coated with the deadly juice again. He crouched down over Delia, who was still flat on his back in the chair, his black eyes wide. Brett put his knee on Delia's chest.

"I don't have much time," the Ninja Master said quickly. "Why did you hire Schenkman?"

"Who the hell are you?" Delia shouted back, raising his head.

Brett used the wakizashi to hack off Delia's right foot. "Tell me!" he demanded.

The sudden dismemberment came as an unbelievable shock. Delia couldn't believe the man in black actually did it, then he couldn't believe the electric vibration coursing through his whole body.

"He came to me," Delia babbled, his body in shock from the pain. "He'd gotten the word I wanted something done. He convinced me he could do it. I was impressed."

"Why?"

"He had killers with nothing to lose," Delia rolled on, the words falling over themselves to get out of his mouth. "No one would think that locked-up killers could do anything. And they'd kill themselves if captured.

Schenkman had their faces changed and their finger-prints burned off so they couldn't be traced. It was perfect."

"Almost," said Brett, and used the long sword to chop off Delia's head. He hacked down like a butcher cutting off a chop from a lamb's rib cage. The corporation boss's head dropped neatly off the rest of his body. It rolled back along the top of the chair. It would have thudded to a stop on the carpet if a torrent of blood hadn't suddenly shot out of the neck stump. The river of spitting liquid carried the head along until it bumped up against the hole in the window. Then, as the current shifted to cascade through the opening, the head was carried along.

It turned toward Brett, Delia's eyes and mouth still open. The expression held only amazement that such a thing could happen. Then the head tipped over and fell out of the window, smashing into an unrecognizable pulp seven stories below.

Brett was out of the office before the head had even tipped over. He left the jerking, headless body in the chair and moved out into the dark empty hall. He slowed to a walk, his head down, his eyes closed, his bloody katana still in his hands. He concentrated on whatever movement was still inside the building.

He heard the three he was seeking. Two were in an elevator moving down and one was taking the stairs. Brett ran to the elevator door, bringing up his long sword. The blood on its blade splashed on the ceiling from Brett's strong movement. He then sliced down, getting the blade between the double elevator door. Pushing the blade in, Brett moved it sideways to make a space big enough to insert his left hand in the opening and slipped the katana back into its scabbard with his right.

His right hand then free, he moved it to join the left,

back to back. Brett pushed outward and the doors parted. He instantly leaped forward, letting the doors close behind him as he wrapped himself around the elevator cable. With his hands protected by gloves, he slid and "hand–climbed" down at intervals determined by the degree of friction heat—sliding one story and "hand–climbing" a half-story alternately. Soon his feet touched the elevator ceiling. He closed his eyes again and "felt" the men inside. One was the fat man. It was a toss up as to the other one. Judging from their reactions in the office, Brett guessed it was the greasy-haired one.

The Ninja Master saw the trapdoor in the elevator's roof. But he knew the men inside had guns, and only the brown-haired man was seriously wounded. He considered dropping through the opening and slicing them before they could fire. But if they had their guns up, they might be able to get some shots off even as they did. And the enclosure was so small, the odds were in their favor to hit him.

Subconsciously counting the floors he had passed, Brett knew they'd be arriving in the lobby within seconds. He quickly kneeled on the front of the roof, away from the trapdoor at his right. He silently pulled the katana out and flipped it so that he had the hilt at the bottom of his hand.

He felt the elevator jerk to a stop. He heard the doors open onto the lobby. He heard the men start to move. Then he stabbed down.

The elevator's ceiling was no match for the strong blade. It sliced through the thin metal like it was cardboard and broke the lights and plastic covering beneath. The tip sunk perfectly into the middle of the smaller man's greasy hair.

And his skull was no match for the blade, either. The

sword sunk down through his brain, behind his eyes, past his nose, through his mouth and deep into his throat. All the fat man knew was that the greasy-haired man had suddenly stopped on their way out of the elevator.

"Come on," he said irritably, not even noticing the tinkle of the broken light bulb on the elevator floor. He glanced back and did a double take. A thin piece of metal had grown out of the greasy-haired killer's head and broken through the elevator ceiling. As he watched, the blade popped out of his head and disappeared. The greasy-haired man made an "urk" noise and fell forward.

The fat man lifted his gun and emptied it into the elevator ceiling. Then he ran as fast as he could for the front door. Brett had already climbed up and forced open the elevator doors on the second floor. The bullets splattered on the shaft wall behind him. Then he ran to the emergency exit and the stairs behind it. He walked out onto the second floor landing, just as the brown-haired man was rounding the third.

As soon as he saw the man in black, the brown-haired man turned to run back the way he had come. He only vaguely heard the hum behind him as Brett unslung his kyotetsu-shoge and whirled the double-edged blade in the air like a lariat at the killer who was trying to get back up the stairs. The knife sunk into his pants and burrowed right up his sphincter. It sliced through and settled deep in his intestines. Brett had given the man a steel enema.

With a tug, Brett pulled the man across the steps as if he were hauling in a fish. The man crashed down the stairs, screaming as he went. His broken wrist was held tightly to his chest, but that didn't prevent it being further smashed against the steps as he fell. Finally he slid onto the second floor landing at Brett's feet.

The Ninja Master was unmoved by his red, sobbing face. Vindictively, he pulled the double-edged blade out of the man's asshole and spun it down to open a gash from the man's navel to his thighs. The man's penis was cut in two as was everything else. All his torso's guts began to fall out of the hole Brett had made.

The brown-haired man screamed horribly as Brett nonchalantly put the kyotetsu-shoge back on his shoulder. He tried to crawl away as Brett leaned down toward him, but his guts were going in one direction as he was moving in the other. He hastily stopped and tried to hold his organs in. Brett nimbly plucked the .357 out of the man's waistband. He continued to scream and bleed, and he died as Brett left the landing, ran back into the building, and toward the front windows.

When he was ten feet away, Brett emptied the revolver into the window. The sound of the shots and breaking glass stopped the fat man for a second. He turned to see Brett's silhouette in the cracked pane. The sight drove him to speeds he had never achieved before. He raced back to the Sanctuary's car in record time and wrenched the door open. At that moment, Brett was bursting through the office building's damaged window. He fell two stories and hit the ground, tumbling. He came up on his feet, running.

The fat man slammed the car door and tried to get his hands on the keys in his pocket, but he was too fat to reach them in that position. He pushed up with his legs, straightening his back across the top of the seat. At the same time, Brett had leaped onto the hood of a car about a hundred feet behind the fat man. Finally, the fat man got his fingers around the keys in his pocket. As he desperately pulled, the keys sprang out from between the cloth and his roll of fat, only to slip out of his sweaty hand. They bounced off the edge of the seat and fell to the floor mat on the passenger's side. The fat man leaned down to get them.

That move saved his life. He heard a crackle and a thunk. When he rose again, two spikes had sunk all the way down to their heads in the seat where he had been sitting. The fat man immediately ducked down again, jamming the key into its cylinder. He twisted as he heard more cracking glass and spinning noises inside the car.

The engine roared to life. But before the fat man put it into gear, he reached under the front seat. When he came up, a sawed-off shotgun was in his hands and Brett was on the roof of the car right in front of him.

It was a point-blank shot. The fat man pulled both triggers. His windshield exploded, the rear windshield of the car parked in front of him exploded and Brett disappeared. The fat man didn't wait. As soon as the triggers were depressed, he let go of the gun, twisted the wheel, moved the clutch and put his foot to the floor. The car's rear wheels squealed and sent up clouds of white, pungent smoke. The front of the Sanctuary vehicle rammed the back end of the buckshot-filled car in front of it. The fat man's car pushed the blocking auto out of the way and then screeched out onto the Santa Cruz street.

Brett rose from his prone position on the sidewalk, a shuriken in his hand. A feeling of déjà vu flitted over him as he remembered doing the same thing at the diner. He brought his arm back and threw the five-pointed star sideways at the rear wheel.

Nothing happened. Brett suddenly realized that these wheels were different than the ones he had seen before. These wheels were not inflated, they were all rubber!

His shuriken merely sunk in and held there. The car had been outfitted with the special tires for such an eventuality. The other killers had been expendable. These three had been important.

A chill ripped across the back of Brett's neck. His equilibrium had been thrown off. The main killer was getting away and there seemed to be nothing he could do about it. Keeping his eye on the receding Sanctuary car, Brett drove his hand through the side window of a 1977 Chevy parked in front of the damaged auto. He lifted the lock, opened the door, and slid in. At the same time, he sliced across the dashboard with his short sword. Dropping the blade on the seat, he drove his hands into the hole and hot-wired the engine, using his fingernails as pliers.

The engine roared to life and Brett pulled out after the fat man. It was lucky that the hour was late and the streets were empty. Brett kept his eyes and ears open, easily following the car's trail. But no matter how well he drove, he could not catch up. The fat man was driving like a man possessed. Which was not surprising, Brett decided, considering how mad he actually was.

The main street was soon left behind and the cars were navigating narrow, winding, suburban roads, getting higher and higher into the hills. Brett could pull closer here. In the city, the fat man could weave all over the roads, but he missed some tight turns on these streets, making him back out of the brush and off the shoulders, losing time. Brett, on the other hand, was controlling his vehicle as if he were a part of it.

"Everything is a weapon, if you know how to use it," he remembered his master telling him. "But to make the weapon work, it must become part of you. An extension of your arm, your leg, your mind." Brett had adjusted his thinking to the car's capabilities in the first thirty seconds of driving. Then he pushed the machine to its absolute limits.

He was just coming around a corner in the woods when he saw the fat man's car for the first time since leaving the city. It was tearing up a side road and smashing through a wooden gate. Brett barreled up the grassy incline after it. He lost sight of the Sanctuary car in the spray of dirt, but kept hard on its tail. After two more turns on the bumpy, rocky road, he heard the lead car skid to a halt. Brett stopped immediately as well, not wanting to drive into a possible ambush.

As the Ninja Master snaked out of the Chevy's open side window, he heard the fat man laboriously jump out of his car door. Then came the sounds of the killer huffing and puffing in the opposite direction. But rather than hearing the sounds of the man struggling through the brush which was all around Brett, he heard the man running on what was obviously cut grass and brown dirt.

A sudden warning of impending doom flashed across Brett's brain. He immediately dove into the brush dividing him from his quarry. He emerged at the top of a hill. The doubtful feeling hit him in the pit of the stomach. Stretched out before him was a baseball field, a picnic area, a row of cabins, and a lake. By the water, he saw the unmistakable signs of youthful inhabitants. Next to the Sanctuary's awkwardly parked car was a van which displayed the painted legend: "Farm Camp Windsor."

Brett finally focused on the fat man, who had just slipped into the cabin closest to the water. He was carrying his knife, his revolver, a rifle, and a small hatchet.

*   *   *

The fat man thought he had died and gone to heaven. Stretched out before him were two rows of little girls, snuggled into their little beds, their angelic faces dreaming about sugar and spice and everything nice. Right by the door was a larger bed and a more mature female face resting on the pillow. The fat man gently took the edge of the sheet covering her and slowly pulled it back. He had to bite his lip to keep from laughing with joy. The receding sheet exposed a beautiful teenage counselor millimeter by millimeter.

She had a head of curly brown hair, a balcony you could recite Shakespeare from, almost no waist at all, strong, rounded hips, and legs that went up to her neck. And all she was wearing was a T-shirt and panties. The fat man brought the ax up above her head. No, he decided, controlling himself. First things first.

He held the knife against the girl's throat and started tickling her between the legs. She murmured in her sleep and arched her back. She rolled flat on her back and her limbs started moving in pleasure. Then she stiffened. Her eyes popped open. When she tried to sit up, the fat man grabbed her hair and pressed the blade tightly against her throat. Her mouth opened, but only a rush of air came out.

"Scream," he quietly told her. "Scream louder than you've ever screamed before."

The sound practically shook the rafters and reverberated through the whole camp. All the children inside the cabin woke up and automatically looked at their counselor. They saw a big man holding her in a very embarrassing way with a hunting knife against her breast. They all started screaming too, their immature voices turning the cabin's interior into an aural hell.

Some kids at the other end of the cabin even tried to

run out of the second door there, but the fat man was too fast for them. He pulled his hand from between the counselor's legs, grabbed his rifle, and sent a bullet right into the middle of the door. Its cracking bark pushed the nearby tots away and cut off all the shrieks. Everyone stared at the big man who held the sobbing girl, their eyes blinking.

"Everybody out of bed!" he roared. "Get into the middle of the room. Now!"

"Please!" the counselor pleaded. "Do as he says."

The fifteen little girls in the cabin hastily did what their counselor asked. They ran together in the center of the floor.

"On your knees," the fat man demanded, waving his rifle at them. "Huddle together. Real close." The little girls responded until they were but a mass of pink flesh in the middle of the floor. The fat man laughed with honest pleasure. He put his knife away and lifted the counselor with one arm around her waist. He walked over to the crowd of girls, brandishing his rifle. When he threw the counselor on the bed in front of the girls, a din of displeasure started up again.

"Shut up!" he screamed, taking his place between the bed and the girls. The interior quieted immediately. "Hey!" he called up to the rafters. "Hey, sword man!"

Brett stood motionless outside the door of the cabin. To the many other campers who were awakened by the din, he was invisible. He did not reply to the fat man.

"Nobody come in here, you hear me?" the fat man continued anyway. "I got a couple of dozen little girls in here with me and I'll kill them if anybody tries to get me. You understand?"

Brett remained motionless. His eyes were closed, but

he listened with his entire body. "Understood," he said quietly.

The fat man heard him inside. "Okay," he continued, relishing every second. "You've got five minutes to get the hell out of here and take everybody else with you. In five minutes I'm coming out with all these girls around me, so you better not try anything or they'll get it first."

At the mention of murder, the little girls began to whisper, gasp, and cry. But they did it very quietly so the fat man didn't do anything about it.

"Five minutes!" the fat man finished with a howl.

Brett heard it in the distance as he ran up to the front of the crowd which had gathered thirty feet away from the cabin. He pulled off his hood as he approached. The people reacted as if his head had appeared out of thin air.

"Quiet," he demanded, using the art of kiai, controlling his voice's strength. The stunned group immediately complied. "You heard him," Brett went on. "Get everybody inside another cabin and don't come out until six minutes are up."

"Shouldn't we call the police?" said one male counselor.

"You do, and the girls will die," Brett answered with conviction. "I know this madman. Call the police after the six minutes are up." He slipped the hood back on and ran back to the cabin in question.

The rest of the campers didn't think twice about Brett's instructions. They did what they were told. That was the power of kiai. Later, no two people could give the police the same description of the disembodied head. And incredibly, no one had the description right anyway.

Inside, the girls steeled themselves for the three hundred sixty seconds of waiting. The fat man had other things he wanted to do with the time. Well, he told himself, it looked like he'd be able to recreate one of his favorite horror movies after all.

"Hey," he said to the cringing girl on the bed. "You." The teenager looked up. "What's your name?" he asked, pointing the knife at her.

"Lucille," she said in a small voice, looking fearfully at him.

"Lucy, huh?" he replied. "Juicy Lucy, huh? Well, Juicy Lucy, you ever heard of a movie called 'Friday the 13th'?"

The look on her face told him she had. The fat man stood in between the bed and the huddled children, his rifle pointed at the kids and his knife on the counselor.

"Well, that movie was about a camp just like this one," he said. "Remember the scene where the two counselors are making it on the bed? Well, listen, Juicy, why don't you recreate that little number for us while we wait?"

"I can't," she said fearfully.

"Why not?" the fat man asked, licking his lips and keeping the most innocent expression on his porcine face.

"My . . . my boyfriend isn't here."

The fat man looked around as if saying, "Now where has that lad gone off to?" Then he looked back at Lucille, his eyes sparkling. "Use this, then," he told her, swinging his rifle around to knock a half empty Coca-Cola bottle off the little night stand next to the bed. It landed with a hollow thud and unmercifully didn't break. The copper-colored liquid began to course out onto the floor. "Well, go on!" he yelled, moving the knife closer to her chest.

Lucille yelped in terror and jerked back onto the bed. Her fear petrified her until all she could do was hold her hands up and cry.

"Do I have to do everything?" the fat man drawled

with exaggerated exasperation. He leaned over and scooped up the soda bottle with his knife hand and poured out the rest of the Coke. It spread out on the floor and seeped into the cracks between floorboards. He then shoved it into Lucille's hands.

"Lie down," the fat man instructed, a dangerous timbre in his voice. Lucille laid back tremulously. "Take the bottle." She fumbled for it and held it against her stomach. "Rub it against your cunt." She shook her head. "Do it!" he screamed.

Her hand jerked out over her crotch in reaction to his hysteria. Then slowly, crying pitiously, she began to rub the top of the bottle against her panties.

The little girls closed their eyes, shielded their faces, and looked away. Most were crying, but some were too numbed to find the tears.

"Harder," the fat man said. "Faster." He was getting really excited now. What he didn't tell her, but what she might have already known, was that this scene ended in the gruesome death of both lovers. In the movie, a spear went through both boy and girl from above. But since the fat man didn't have a spear, the knife would have to do.

He moved closer to the girl as she struggled on the bed, her eyes closed and head to the side, crying bitter tears. Although the cabin was illuminated by only one light— the one the fat man had turned on upon entering—his face was nearly glowing with homicidal power. He was in complete control, giving reality to his sickest fantasy.

In spite of her torment, the girl's body was beginning to respond to her forced stimulation. The fat man saw that her breathing was heavier and was jerking in time with her interior contractions. It was only a matter of moments before she came, he realized. And that moment of her greatest feeling was the moment he would plunge the knife into her.

He took purposeful step after purposeful step toward her writhing form almost losing all track of the rifle in his maniacal passion. Lucille's mouth opened and began to make little noises as his knife poised over her bucking form.

Her mouth widened, her back arched and she pressed the bottle hard against herself. The fat man raised his knife quickly.

The entire bed fell over. Propelled by a force underneath, the mattress and frame swung up and over on to its left side. The girl was thrown to the floor and the bed fell on top of her. Rising in its place was Brett Wallace.

The camp cabin was a classic structure made of logs. Since it was built as cheaply and practically as possible, it had no foundation. Rather, it was built upon a wooden frame which simply gave its carpenters a flat level to construct upon. Brett had cut a hole in this frame, crawled underneath and waited for the fat man to give his exact location away by his footsteps. Brett silently made a hole with his wakizashi, then stood up at the opportune moment. He had to wait until the fat man was close enough so he could be disarmed without harming the children.

Brett was not subtle in his disarmament. The knife was still coming down when he rose up. He merely put his blade about a foot above where the girl had been. The fat man was unable to slow his thrust. His arm went right into and through the Ninja Master's sword. He watched his limb fall into the hole Brett had made, still tightly clutching the knife.

The fat man reared back, bellowing as his stump

sprayed blood and the screaming little girls dashed in all directions. The fat man tried to turn and aim his rifle. Brett sprang out of the hole and drew his katana at lightning speed. Taking it out of the scabbard served as the first blow. As the sword sped around in an arc, the fat man's other arm was cut off at the elbow. The gun and forearm slammed to the floor and skidded to the opposite wall. Now both the fat man's arms were spewing the cabin with blood. The killer's mind was on automatic alarm. He kept up one steady howl as he stumbled around and tried to charge out the door.

Both of Brett's swords were back in their scabbards. But the kyotetsu-shoge was off his shoulder and buzzing like a nest of hornets. Only he didn't throw the end with the double-edged blade. He had a different fate in mind for the fat man. He hurled the weighted end of the elastic, which wrapped around the killer's neck, grew taut, and brought the fat man down like a beached whale.

Still holding on to one end of the kyotetsu-shoge with one hand, Brett threw the bed and mattress off the counselor. He gently lifted her to her feet by the elbow.

"Are you all right?" he asked. Through tears, she nodded. "He won't get away with this," he promised her. "Now get out of here and don't look back into this place until they've cleaned it up." Lucille didn't need any more coaxing. She ran around the room gathering the frightened children and led them all outside. Brett smiled grimly inside his hood. At least he managed to save one girl who might grow up as kind and strong as she seemed now. The fat man deserved a death befitting his life.

Brett pulled on the elastic strand, moving the fat man toward him. The killer was still yelling and trying to get his feet under him without the use of his gushing arm stumps. Brett had faith in him. He knew the fat man's insanity would give him the strength to stay conscious until after Brett dealt with him.

The two adversaries met halfway. The fat man's face was awash with blood, what was left of his arms useless at his side. Brett stood two feet from him, holding the elastic cord like a leash. Brett read it on the killer's face before it happened. He saw that the man was gathering himself for one last attack. When the fat man charged, Brett was ready.

Both swords appeared in his hands as he dropped the cord. Both swords jerked in and through the fat man's chest as he surged forward. Then, before the madman had even realized that he had been pierced, the blades were out again and Brett was twisting around to the back.

The fat man's momentum was not interrupted. He continued to lurch forward. Brett planted his feet and dove both swords into the obese body from the rear, both points coming out of the fat man's chest. Before he could look down and see them, Brett had pulled them out and thrown them into the cabin's wood floor. They stuck in the wood on either side of the Ninja Master as he sped toward the slowing porcine figure.

Just before he reached him, Brett's right hand shot out, his palm open, his fingers forming a spearhead which smashed into the fat man's back. With his swords, Brett had made a small square running through the killer's body. He had done it so quickly and so perfectly that hardly any internal organs were displaced. The various veins and nerves were severed, but Brett had three seconds before the fat man's mind told his body about the loss.

In that three seconds, Brett's karate powered hand went almost all the way through the fat man's body, pushing everything inside the square he had cut out through the killer's chest. The fat man felt the wrenching pressure and looked down just as most of his heart erupted from between his tits. He moved to catch the guts but he had no hands left to catch them with. He watched his heart fall onto the floor with a splat. Then he fell face first onto it, seeing nothing.

Chapter Seven

The first guard never knew what hit him. He merely leaned back in his chair and died. He hadn't even seen the shuriken which came sizzling out of the woods and through the shack's one open window. He was just becoming aware of an unusual hum when one of the weapon's edges sunk into his forehead. His head fell back and he remained in his chair, his feet flat on the floor.

The death of the second guard was a little more complicated. They had replaced the wizened old man with a younger fellow who kept moving inside the shack. Taken alone, his energy wouldn't have been a problem, but Brett had to get through two fences in addition. So he moved a bit closer and retrieved one of his poisoned dirks from his shoulder holder. Lining things up and anticipating the guard's movements, Brett threw the blade straight.

It went through the links of the first fence perfectly and

just nicked the side of the second fence. But coming off that contact were crackles of electricity and some sparks. They had electrified the fence and that threw the dirk's trajectory off completely. The blade slammed into the rear wall of the second shack, just chopping a lock off the guard's hair.

The man leaped for his phone. He had the receiver to his ear and his finger poised on the alert button when Brett's second dirk sank into the back of his neck, cutting his spinal column. He fell backward, driving the point in deeper, and tearing the receiver right out of the phone box.

Brett circled the outside fence. He saw the wire running from the generator to the fence in back. It was the same location where the Sanctuary wall was closest to the inside fence. Brett decided to scale it there. He checked the horizon. It was only a few minutes before dawn—almost twenty-four hours since Brett made his first visit to Dr. Schenkman. Wallace turned away from the inspiring sight and trudged back into the woods.

He found a strong, fairly straight, long branch which would serve his purposes. He made sure all his weapons were secure and then ran forward, the branch held out in front of him in both hands. He jabbed its far end into the ground in front of the first fence, and vaulted over, not letting go of his makeshift pole. The second fence was a bit trickier. He had to vault over from a diagonal so when he let the stick go it would not hit the electrified fence.

Brett mentally worked out the equations and angle, while checking to see if he were still in the blind spot in front of the section of the wall which had no windows. Pulling the stick up again, he ran parallel to the second fence, planted the branch end and soared up, his muscular legs giving him the height he needed. He let go of the stick too soon from an athlete's point of view, but his momentum carried him over while the stick fell between the two fences without touching either.

Brett hit the grass, somersaulted, and came up in a crouch, running. He ran until he reached the very back wing of the asylum—the section where he assumed they kept what Dr. Parker called "the dangerous ones." He leaped up onto the wall next to a large, linked-in window. His ninja-trained fingers dug into the rough surface of the brick-and-concrete wall and held him there as if he had been coated with Krazy Glue. He inched over to the window like a human fly and looked in.

The fluorescent light from within revealed a macabre scene. Instead of beds, Brett saw two lines of tables, vaguely resembling the rows of beds back at the camp. They were similar in shape and the fact they had people on them covered to the neck with white sheets. But even at this distance, Brett could tell that these people were not breathing. His conclusion was further enhanced by the presence of bodies on the floor between the tables and against the walls.

There wasn't even an attempt to place these corpses in an orderly fashion. They just lay where they were dropped, their gaping wounds caked with blood and infested with flies. Some of these victims wore uniforms, some wore suits, and some even wore hospital gowns.

Brett hastily moved to the window's corner. Pulling a spike from his ankle holder, he jammed its edge between the wall and the nailed metal link covering. With a twist, he had pulled the securing nail out of the wall. He bent the fencing back and dropped in between it and the window.

The window was a large type that pulled in at the

bottom rather than sliding up. Not surprisingly, it wasn't locked. The people inside weren't going anywhere.

Brett dropped down into the room proper. It had the stench of a morgue during a power failure. The air was dank with a putrid smell and flies flitted from corpse to corpse. Brett walked among the dead, awed by the casual way they were dumped into their respective spots. By the amount of blood outside their bodies and other general clues, he surmised that they had been killed elsewhere and moved into this room. From what he could gather, the executions had started slowly and then built in tempo and viciousness.

The people on the tables seemed peaceful in death. Those on the floor were mutilated more and their faces were mingled with expressions of pain and fear. Strangely, it was the male corpse on the last table—the one closest to the freezer-like door—which had the most tortured expression. Brett was drawn to this body out of curiosity. Judging by its state of rigor mortis and decomposition, it was the oldest corpse.

The eyes were wide and glassy. The nostrils were flared. The lips were twisted and the brow was tight. Strangely, Brett didn't find himself thinking that the victim had been horrified by his own death. Somehow, the corpse's expression held a paternal, samaritan's fear—the fear of danger to others. Brett couldn't be sure whether these thoughts came from the dead, frozen face, or from his own mind—where a solution to all the monstrous killings was beginning to take form.

Brett studied the body further. The man had gray hair, still neatly coiffed. He had a mustache that had been expertly trimmed. There were definite signs of strangulation across his neck. Strangulation by a strong, experienced garroter. Brett pulled the sheet back. The man was still clothed. His shirt was a fashionable light green while his slacks were expensive tweed. His shoes were handsome leather oxfords. On the fourth finger of his right hand was a ring.

Brett lifted the hand with the ring to his eyes. It was a large ring with a blue stone on it from some fraternal medical organization. On one side of the stone was a date—1963—and on the other side were initials—"R. M. S." Brett laid the hand back down, his eyes rising to the point where the wall met the ceiling. A heinous theory crossed his mind. It was a truly nasty, disgusting chain of events Brett imagined, but all the pieces fit.

The Ninja Master looked around the room as if he suddenly realized where he was, his face set in a determined, deadly expression. His steel-gray eyes turned cold and his blood ran like a river struck by a monsoon. He ran back to the window and climbed up, slipping through the broken corner of the protecting mesh, then pulled himself all the way to the Sanctuary roof. He stood as the sun was just sending its initial rays up over the distant hills. The black sky was tempered by blue in the east and the horizon was lined with a dark green.

The Ninja Master's steps were not heard inside. His movements were not seen or felt by any living thing. He passed through the middle of a flock of birds and not one took flight. He traveled over the top of the asylum until he came to the edge of the roof above Schenkman's office. He lowered himself onto the wall with his hands, sliding down the surface feet first. Then he let go of the roof's edge as his toes dug in, and he started to descend to the doctor's unprotected picture window.

He stopped when he heard voices. He held himself just to the side and above the glass as his acute hearing picked up the sounds coming through.

"They're late," said a strained, female voice.

"I'm well aware of that," said a strident male voice in return. "But Keith might have gone off on a tangent. You know how he is."

"I wish I didn't," said the woman, obviously Claire Dearborne. Brett could tell she was shuddering. "The others are getting restless."

"The natives are getting restless, eh?" Schenkman responded. "It's just excitement. You've seen it before."

"Not like this," the nurse professed. "I don't know if I can control them."

"*I* can," said the doctor with fervent certainty. "Where are they?"

"In the therapy room. As you ordered."

"Excellent," Schenkman extolled. Brett heard him rising from his chair. "Tonight is their night. It is the culmination of everything I've worked for. Before the evening is out, there will be untold excitement."

"What if Keith doesn't show?" Dearborne said in a worried tone. "You told him this would be the last one. What if he just takes the final payment and runs?"

The next words chilled Brett's blood. "It doesn't matter," Schenkman said quietly. "It makes no difference anymore. Nothing does."

With that, Brett heard the doctor sweep out of the room. Nurse Dearborne hesitantly followed. As soon as their footsteps receded in the distance, Brett crawled closer to the window. He checked its entire circumference for alarms. There were none. Another cost-saving decision, no doubt, Brett thought. Brett's only other problem getting in was that Schenkman's window was not constructed to open.

Brett put the flat of his hand on the corner closest to him. He pushed until a crack began to form. He kept pushing until the crack reached two other edges of the frame and then a triangular piece of the glass fell in. Brett had broken off the upper left section of the window. There was enough room for him to let go of the wall with his hands completely and dive into the office, using his gripping feet on the wall as springboards.

The glass had bounced, and then broken with a tiny tinkle on the thickly carpeted floor. Brett somersaulted beyond it, coming up against the far wall. He listened at the door carefully to make sure no one had been alerted by his entrance. If anything, the administrative hallway was quieter than ever.

Brett pulled open the door and looked outside. The hall was bleak and dismal, lit by a line of flourescent ceiling fixtures, giving the area a morbid yellow glow. As far as Brett could tell, not a creature was stirring on this side of the far door. To take advantage of the situation, he moved from Schenkman's office to the door nearest him on the right. But like all the others in this wing, it was closed.

It opened easily at Brett's pull however, revealing an empty office. It looked like it had been occupied at one time, but a layer of dust had built up on the various pieces of furniture and accoutrements. Brett's memory brought back a picture of the corpses on the tables in the wing across the asylum. He counted them in his mind, and then counted the number of closed offices. Including Schenkman's, there were nine offices. Including the gray-haired corpse with the ring, there were nine bodies on the tables.

Brett's body was suddenly fueled by a desperate drive of energy that told him that if he didn't stop it completely, the worst atrocity was yet to come. He ran to the far door, listening all the while for the guard who should have been there. He saw no one on this side and no evidence of anyone nearby on the other. The door itself was not locked. It swung open easily.

The hall of "harmless" psychos was empty. But in the distance, Brett could hear a buzzing roar of activity. He could feel the energy in the air, crackling around his head in an oppressive grip. Removing both his swords from their scabbards, he moved down through the shadows at the side of the hall. As he went, the sound got louder and louder. He was nearing the therapy room.

The Ninja Master stopped outside the main entrance to the Sanctuary building itself. Something in the lobby office caught his eye. Walking backward toward it, keeping most of his concentration on the hall where the noise was coming from, Brett backed up against the windowed door of the receiving area. Glancing over his shoulder he saw that instead of incoming patients, the chairs and tables inside the dark lobby were covered with weapons.

Pistols, rifles, boxes of ammo, axes, knives, and even machetes were lying around the room, waiting for someone to use them. And there was one thing more. Along the back wall was a row of red metal cans.

Brett instantly chopped off the door knob. He had no more time for finesse. Pushing the other knob inside the room out of the way, he stuck a gloved finger in the mechanism and pushed the obstruction aside. He ran to the far wall first and unscrewed one of the can's tops. With a sniff, he knew all the tins contained gasoline. Brett didn't care why they were here with the weapons. He just intended to make good use of them.

Tipping the first can, he doused the area liberally with the volatile liquid. He kept pouring until he had formed a pool in the middle of the room. Dropping the can on a sofa next to a dozen rifles, he pulled the last spike out of his ankle holder. He threw that into the floor at the very edge of the pool of gas so that most of the spike's length was still visible.

Then, whipping out his long sword, he raised it high above his head. Cutting swiftly down, he nicked the edge of the spike, sending out three sparks. A ring of fire suddenly blazed in the middle of the room. Brett was out the door before the first flame licked the ceiling. Throwing caution to the winds, he raced down the hall toward the therapy room, the long hanging lights bathing him in a yellow glow as he went.

He moved into the shadows as he neared the room. He could see the entrance was packed with people, and just as many seemed to be crammed inside. From his angle along the far wall, Brett got the impression that the therapy room was a combination gym and sauna. He could see the edges of a vaulting "horse," parallel bars, and a whirlpool machine. He could also hear the strong voice of Schenkman inspiring his fellows.

"Tonight is the culmination of everything we've worked for!" he declared triumphantly. The crowd responded with a raucous cheer. "This may be the end of our reign here, but it is just the beginning of our reign out there!" The crowd really went wild. Schenkman waited until the babble quieted down.

"When you leave here tonight," he continued when the room had gone deathly quiet, "you will be presented with one thousand dollars, a gun, a knife, and transportation." At least that explained the weapons and gas cans, Brett thought. Schenkman didn't want the cars stopping for gas until they reached their destinations. "Each of you will be given an area to survive in, and each of you will survive the best way he knows how!"

The group laughed at that. A knowing, chattering

laughter. Schenkman didn't wait for the mirth to subside this time. He rolled right over it. "You will be free!" he cried. "For the first time in your lives, you will be free. Free to live, and . . ."—he said this last part knowingly— ". . . free to die."

Brett remembered the laughing faces of the attackers who had committed suicide before his eyes, and he understood what Schenkman was saying. These people were walking time bombs. They could go off anytime, dying in the process, but taking a lot of innocents with them. Brett's lips were set grimly. He had a time bomb of his own.

The crowd inside the therapy room was roaring its approval when the overhead sprinklers went on. The cheer was cut off as the cascades of rain came down. They looked up in confusion just as the fire alarm sounded and the front of the Sanctuary exploded.

The entrance doors, windows, and part of the wall blew out in all directions with the force of a guided missile. The blast spread out, ripping through the building as well as littering the front lawn with debris. The therapy room was shaken and the occupants thrown about. Immediately after, most of the room emptied to hastily investigate the situation. They all missed Brett, who had leaped up to the overhead, rectangular lighting fixture. He hid on the top as the majority of the crazies ran underneath. As they turned the corner at the end of the hall, Brett dropped down.

Inside the therapy room, Schenkman was standing on an upraised stage at the far end of the room. He was visibly shaken, but not as much as Dearborne, who had pressed herself back in the corner, a look of horror on her face. The more confused of the psychos remained in various positions in the room around the padded horse, parallel bars, trapeze, whirlpool machines, walkers, and climbing ropes. The floor was hardwood and covered with mattresses and pads.

Brett charged inside, both swords swinging. His first katana swing cut across the back of a man's head without him knowing it. Brett chopped down across a nearby man's profile with his short blade at the same time. He leaped between both men as they fell. While still in midair, he thrust forward with the long blade, piercing a man's neck who was facing him. The wakizashi jerked to the side and came up under the sternum of a man who had moved toward the racing ninja.

Brett hit the floor with both feet in front of the parallel bars. His swords slipped back into his scabbards even as he was jumping high into the air. He somersaulted in space and landed with each foot on a different parallel bar. He ran forward on these, balancing perfectly. Two men reached for him, but missed as he dove off the end and grabbed one of the suspended climbing ropes.

He swung all the way across the rest of the room and landed on the platform between Schenkman and Dearborne, his swords already out of the scabbards and in his hands. The short sword was pointed at the doctor and the long blade faced those remaining on the therapy room floor.

"Get out," he told the nurse over his shoulder. "You have the diversion. Get out now." Dearborne didn't move. "You have no idea what they're planning," he pleaded with her. "You're expendable. Get out now."

"I'm scared," came her tiny voice behind him. "Shield me. Protect me."

"Come on," he said, moving toward the edge of the platform by sliding his feet along the stage in that direction. He kept one eye on the stunned crazies below and one on the doctor, who was looking at him with fervent rage. But there was something more on Schenkman's face. It was an impassioned expression of superiority. Even though Brett had mowed down many of his men, he was still looking at Brett as if he—the doctor— were the winner.

A sudden realization flooded Brett's brain, but it was already too late for him to do anything about it. As the possible explanation occurred to him, the proof of his new theory struck him from behind.

Brett felt the needle slam into his back between his shoulder blades. Dearborne had taken the syringe in both hands and slammed it into him, one fist pushing the plunger.

Brett staggered toward Schenkman, realizing his mistake. He had believed Dearborne when she said that she knew nothing of Schenkman's plans. He believed her when she said she was only doing it for the money. He believed her to be a greedy, ambitious person, but he also believed that she would ultimately become a victim. It was only at the last second that he convinced himself that she could be one of "them."

Brett felt the drug spreading out in his back muscles as he fell to his knees. He held onto his swords with white knuckled fists as he dropped forward to rest on all fours. He became aware of laughter above him. Large, purple orbs were beginning to fill his vision, but he was still aware of the shoes that stepped to either side of his outstretched katana blade.

"Idiot," he heard Schenkman say. "Imagine. Trying to take on all of us. And with two swords too." The doctor tsked, then reached down and pulled off Brett's ninja hood.

He stood and casually threw the hood off the platform.

Brett's head stayed bowed, his misting eyes still on the floor. "Poor, stupid Mr. Wallace," Schenkman clucked. "Our little Ms. Dearborne took you completely in, did she? Well, she has that talent, Mr. Wallace. That she certainly does."

Brett had been wrong. The bitter realization filled him with remorse. He had been so sure of his lie-detecting talents, he had neglected to remember that lie detectors could be wrong. He forgot that people besides ninja adepts could control their emotional responses. He failed to take into account that Dearborne could be as insane in her way as Schenkman was in his. And with insanity came reserves of strength "normal" humans were rarely able to tap.

"What you didn't know," Schenkman was lecturing him, "was that Ms. Dearborne was a friend of mine. And what you didn't know was that *I am not Robert Schenkman!*"

Brett remembered the ring on the gray-haired corpse's finger with the initials "R.M.S." They stood for "Robert Merrill Schenkman."

"You see," the fake Schenkman affably continued. "Ms. Dearborne and I went on a little spree last year. We killed three pairs of necking lovers along the west coast, didn't we Claire?" The nurse smiled behind Brett. "Actually, I should say I killed them. She watched. So the police caught me and never knew that a nurse had been aiding and abetting their alleged perpetrator.

"Well sir, I convinced them that I was crazy. It wasn't hard. You come up with any stupid story about God telling you to punish the wicked and even the worst lawyer can make a plea of insanity stick. So they sent me to a maximum security hospital. And when I didn't do anything wrong for a year, they sent me here."

163

The fake doctor turned away from Brett, continuing with his story, secure in the knowledge that Brett was helpless. Dearborne had brought the injections along in case any of the others got too excited. It was a serum which would paralyze the patient, then knock him cold. He fought it, but he was losing all touch with reality. The only thing inside his head was the fake Schenkman's torrent of words.

"They were *wonderful* here!" the man gushed. "All they cared about was you. They wouldn't let the police bother you, they wouldn't let any of the victims' families bother you. They hardly bothered you. And if you were good, and got along with everybody real well, they'd let you out on furloughs once a week. To 'reaccustom oneself to the outside world.' To 'make one's reentry into society as easy as possible.'"

Brett had heard of places like these. Psychiatric hospitals with a "revolving door" parole policy. No matter what your sentence was or for how long, they'd let even known homicidal people out, alone, to buy something they said they needed.

"It was like a vacation," the fake Schenkman professed. "Except I suddenly found that a good number of the patients here—not most of them, but a solid minority— were *just like me*. They were mass murderers who had convinced the courts that they were unfit to stand trial. The place was full of them. We outnumbered the doctors!"

These men were insane, Brett rationalized, but they were not crazy. He held that there was a deadly distinction: crazy men were uncontrollable; the insane killers among them were all but too controllable. They had set out, for their own reasons—anything from getting kicks to "I don't like Mondays"—to kill those who bothered them. And almost everybody did.

"So I got to thinking," the fake doctor carried on. "Why just loll around? Why not pay back society in spades? Why not do what the Sanctuary was so hot for? Why not let everybody reenter society? Ah, but why not do it in style? I wasn't anxious to 'reenter society.' There'd be nothing I'd like better than to go away somewhere with my lady and do anything I wanted for the rest of my life.

"But that takes money, man. So I figured, why not? I knew all the 'hits' that were going down from my contacts. And what I didn't know, my friends here did. So, on one of my furloughs I visited Franklin Delia and we set up a package deal. All we had to do then was kill all the doctors and the patients who wouldn't go along with our little plan. Then we were set."

"Except that's when Nurse McDonald showed up," Dearborne reminded him.

"Yeah," he said slowly. "That fucking temporary nurse. Schenkman had hired her for a stint—from over the phone—before I killed him. I didn't know about it until she showed up. We couldn't just kill her then and there. At the very least the company she worked for would ask questions. So we let her do her work. We decided to kill her afterward and make it look like a random murder. But we had to do it before she might trip over a picture or description of what the real Schenkman looked like."

"But you got in the way," Dearborne spat at the quaking man on his hands and knees.

"But not for very much longer," the murderer promised. "Soon you'll lose consciousness from the drug. Then we'll be happy to make you the first victim of our liberating revolution." He looked from Brett to Dearborne. "Go get the others," he instructed her. She moved toward the edge of the stage. "And shut the fucking sprinklers off!" he yelled after her.

The blond girl hopped off the level and ran out. The fake Schenkman returned to where Brett was, kneeled down and lifted Wallace's head with a cupped hand under his chin. Brett was blinking, sweat pouring across his face.

"Allow me to introduce myself," the killer said pleasantly. "My real name is Kenneth Christian. Pleased to meet you." He dropped Brett's chin and rose to his full height above the shaking man. "The plan was perfect. We worked so fast that Schenkman didn't have to make an appearance at the Frisco hospital where he worked once a week. So no one knew I had taken his place. For any calls, Schenkman was 'in conference.' No visitors were allowed. Even if they complained to the state, by the time *they* got around to doing anything about it, we'd be long gone.

"Yes, my fine doomed friend. The Sanctuary was more than a home away from home. It was an open door. Our punishment for killing was a pat on the head and an open invitation to go out and kill more."

That's right, a part of Brett's mind said. *Keep talking, asshole. Just give me what I need the most. Time.*

Dearborne came running back in, almost everyone else following her. "There's a fucking fire out there!" she announced. "The gasoline went up, and took the guns with it. The others are getting upset." She jumped back onto the stage, moving over to the corner where her syringes and vials lay under a towel.

"Don't worry about it," Christian said. "I can take care of them." He walked to the edge of the stage and lifted his hands. "My friends!" he shouted over the falling water as curls of smoke began to drift into the room. "This was only a diversion! It was the vain, foolish attempt of one man to stop us! But we can buy more guns and our cars wait outside. This man could not stop us. I have him here!"

With a sweep of his arm, Christian pointed at Brett. "He is helpless!" the man called out. "He killed four of your brothers," Christian said, pointing at the corpses whose blood was being washed away by the sprinklers on the ceiling. "But then we defeated him!" Christian marched from one end of the platform to the other. "Who has a weapon?" he demanded.

"Here!" Brett heard a voice which he identified as belonging to "Dr." Parker. The fat killer threw a knife up to his leader. Christian took it and returned to Brett, standing before and above his head, the knife held in a ceremonial position, his feet planted on either side of Brett's sword.

"This man will be the first sacrifice in our struggle to be free! I will strike this blow for freedom myself!"

The crowd cheered. Christian raised his head and voice to the sky. "In the name of the persecuted people, the forgotten people of this world, I send you to a world of everlasting hell!"

Brett stood up before the knife could come down.

As soon as he had felt the drug enter his body, he had slowed his metabolism down and forced his body to become very cold. At the same time he had gulped air, oxygenating his bloodstream to weaken the effect of the drug. He had stayed still, his blood pressure low, until all his fluids were able to pass through his liver, his system's cleansing agent. As soon as the time was up, he forced his metabolism forward in a rush, driving his heartbeat to its extreme limits. All his bodily functions were driven to their maximum, flushing the alien serum out through his pores and into his liver. He was unable to eradicate all the drug's effects, but he remained conscious.

Then he stood, putting all his strength into the hand that held the katana. The sword rose between Christian's legs. It swept up over Brett's head as if Christian had not been in the way. To Dearborne and the audience, it looked as if the samurai sword had magically passed through their leader without making a scratch.

Brett finished his move with a tortured explosion of air pressed through his throat. He stopped motionless with his katana held down at his own feet. He faced the crazies down below, breathing heavily, blocking their view of Christian.

A full five seconds passed with the Ninja Master and the madmen staring silently at each other. Then a wide spray of red erupted from behind Brett, surrounding his body like a glowing crimson cloud. Brett remained still. Following the bloody spray came concentrated gobs which hit the stage with audible thuds. Finally Kenneth Christian's corpse fell to either side behind Brett, his body having been cut cleanly in half—*vertically*.

The crazies gasped as one. Everyone seemed to take a step back. But they saw Brett wasn't doing anything. They stopped until the Ninja Master slowly, carefully, but purposefully, turned toward Claire Dearborne.

The blond girl screamed in deeply felt terror and ran off the edge of the stage. Her fall signaled the others to trample each other in an attempt to get through the rear door. Brett leaped after the girl, both swords flashing in a continual killing motion.

His teeth were gritted and he was growling as he sliced down, up, to the sides and across. Both arms seemed to be moving in distinct opposition to each other, but they never blocked one another. Each twist of the blade caught flesh and dug. No matter how the crazies twisted, jumped, and ducked, the swords found them. Brett hacked through heads, arms, torsos, necks, hips, and legs as he moved through the crowd. Unarmed, terrified, all they could do was fall before his wrath.

The only one with a weapon was Dr. Parker. He fought against the stream of panic-stricken patients, trying to get Brett in the sights of his revolver. He fired it twice, both times hitting a maniac who got in the way. Finally he pushed aside the last of the obstructions. The Ninja Master was ten feet away. He had a clear shot over the whirlpool machine—which was overflowing from the sprinklers.

As he aimed, he became aware that one of Brett's hands was no longer holding a sword. Instead it was bent back. Parker saw the arm extend in his direction, but he wasn't worried since Brett's head was facing a man he was cleaving with his katana.

The gun never went off. Two darts sunk into Parker's eyes. They drove past his nerve endings, their poisoned tips embedding in his brain. He fell forward into the whirlpool machine.

The wakizashi was back in Brett's right hand. He was practically ankle deep in blood and guts now, and the falling water coursed around him. But no matter how slick it got, he did not lose his footing. That was more than could be said about the others, however. They fell and were trampled by the others.

Brett finally made it to the door, having to step over several crushed bodies who had been squashed in the initial rush to escape. Without looking back, Brett swept into the hallway, his swords held out like wings. He saw the rest of the group running into the thick smoke toward the front of the building. Just before she disappeared into this cloud screen, Brett saw the face of Claire Dearborne looking back. He charged forward through the belching mist.

His eyes closed, Brett continued to swing his blades, cutting down by the sense of hearing as he passed. He located the sound of Dearborne's steps in the corner of his mind and followed right on her tail. The smoke cleared a bit near the front. In its stead was incredible heat and orange flame which blocked the exit. But it had yet to block the hallway to the administration wing. Brett heard her feet running in that direction.

With a guttural shout, he leaped up into the air and sailed over the flames, somersaulting above Dearborne's head. He landed fifteen feet in front of her, blocking her path. He held his swords out to his side and smiled. Lovingly. Invitingly.

Dearborne stopped in her tracks and turned around. Behind her was a pack of patients who had gathered together. They didn't look happy.

"You said this couldn't happen!" one shouted at her.

"You said we would be free!" said another.

These men were not the controllable crazies. These were the truly bonkers boys who had to be cajoled, sweet-talked, and even shock-therapied into going along for the ride. They may have seemed pliant to Christian and Dearborne before, but hell hath no fury like a madman cheated.

"Please," she pleaded with them, hands imploringly extended as she glanced over her shoulder at Brett.

"You promised!" said the first crazy with rage.

"You lied to us!" said the second. They all started moving toward her.

The blond turned to stand between the fire and Wallace. She looked from one to the other, then took a last look at the approaching madmen.

Claire Dearborne turned on her left heel and ran into the flames. The crazy men followed in a shouting mass.

Brett turned and ran to Schenkman's office. He passed through the open doorway and soared over the doctor's desk, hitting the unbroken section of the window—his arms protecting his face. He landed on the ground, fell and rolled. For the next five minutes he circled the building around the back, cutting down those who had escaped the therapy room first—the ones who had not already been electrocuted trying to climb the fence.

When he reached the front, Dearborne was already dead. It was not a pretty sight. That which the fire had not burned off was ripped off by the other crazies. They all lay in a smoking mass along the front walk, some still burning.

Brett looked off toward the horizon. It was dawn, and it was beautiful.

The samurai swords fell out of his slack fingers. The remnants of the drug were now released from its oxygenated prison. Brett's eyes rolled up, his lids closed, and he fell unconscious next to Dearborne's body.

Chapter Eight

Brett Wallace was at the San Francisco hospital when Lynn McDonald regained consciousness, but he was not in her room. No one was allowed there. He was on the same couch he had sat on twice before when the doctor approached him.

"I'm sorry," was the first thing the man said. Brett was sure she was dead. It turned out to be a lot worse. "Ms. McDonald has awakened, but I'm afraid there's been brain damage. We don't know how extensive it is yet, but she is not responding to treatment. The damage may be permanent. We just don't know. Only time will tell."

Brett handed the doctor a small package he had taken out of the fat man's car at Farm Camp Windsor. It was the one he had buried in the woods outside the Sanctuary.

"See to it that she gets the best possible help," Brett said softly. "Can I see her?"

Brett was let into room seven-fifteen. Lynn McDonald was propped up with pillows. Her face was beautiful, serene, and empty.

She didn't see Brett at first and when she finally became aware of him, she looked right through him. Brett took her hand. It was warm, but she did not react. He put his other hand over their two.

The only thing that he could tell himself was that this was not his fault. He had not brought the murderers to her. It was not because of him that she was attacked. Without him, she would have been dead. But then another voice in his head answered that maybe she would have been better off that way.

Brett leaned forward and kissed her. He tried everything he could with acupressure to bring her back. There was no response. Brett slowly put her into a serene, restful sleep. He prayed she would wake up from it as if nothing had happened, but he knew that could never come true.

He turned toward Lieutenant Anthony, who was standing in the doorway. "What took you so long?" Brett asked without humor.

Anthony shrugged, coming into the room. "I just happened to be in the neighborhood when the hospital called about checking a large sum of cash they had been given to take care of this patient. I came over personally since I had a little time." He stood next to Brett beside the bed.

Wallace looked back at McDonald's serene face. "Case closed?" he asked lightly.

"No," Anthony replied, "but all of a sudden things have slowed down. The higher-ups are suddenly acting like its not that important to find who killed the Hansens anymore. You wouldn't happen to know anything about that, would you?"

Brett shook his head in the negative. "And you wouldn't happen to know about a mass murder in Santa Cruz a couple of days ago, would you? Where they found seven people slaughtered in a corporate headquarters, one man killed after taking hostages at a camp, an entire asylum for the criminally insane burned to the ground?"

Brett turned his head to look at the policeman. "What do you think?" he asked quietly.

Anthony stared at Brett's gray eyes for a moment, then looked away. "I think you're a very hard man to get to know," he said uncomfortably. "I can't seem to find out anything about you."

"What do you want to know?" Brett asked him, something in his voice scaring Anthony down to his cuticles.

The cop paused for a long, long time.

"Nothing," he said finally. "Absolutely nothing."

5 EXCITING ADVENTURE SERIES
MEN OF ACTION BOOKS

__NINJA MASTER
by Wade Barker
Committed to avenging injustice. Brett Wallace uses the ancient Japanese art of killing as he stalks the evildoers of the world in his mission.
__#3 BORDERLAND OF HELL   *(C30-127, $1.95)*
__#4 MILLION-DOLLOR MASSACRE   *(C30-177, $1.95)*
__#5 BLACK MAGICIAN   *(C30-178, $1.95)*

__THE HOOK
by Brad Latham
Gentleman detective, boxing legend, man-about-town. The Hook crosses 1930's America and Europe in pursuit of perpetrators of insurance fraud.
__#1 THE GILDED CANARY   *(C90-882, $1.95)*
__#2 SIGHT UNSEEN   *(C90-841, $1.95)*
__#5 CORPSES IN THE CELLAR   *(C90-985, $1.95)*

__S-COM
by Steve White
High adventure with the most effective and notorious band of military mercenaries the world has known—four men and one woman with a perfect track record.
__#3 THE BATTLE IN BOTSWANA   *(C30-134, $1.95)*
__#4 THE FIGHTING IRISH   *(C30-141, $1.95)*
__#5 KING OF KINGSTON   *(C30-133, $1.95)*

__BEN SLAYTON: T-MAN
by Buck Sanders
Based on actual experiences, America's most secret law-enforcement agent—the troubleshooter of the Treasury Department—combats the enemies of national security.
__#1 A CLEAR AND PRESENT DANGER *(C30-020, $1.95)*
__#2 STAR OF EGYPT   *(C30-017, $1.95)*
__#3 THE TRAIL OF THE TWISTED CROSS *(C30-131, $1.95)*
__#5 BAYOU BRIGADE   *(C30-200, $1.95)*

__BOXER UNIT—OSS
by Ned Cort
The elite 4-man commando unit of the Office of Strategic Studies whose dare-devil missions during World War II place them in the vanguard of the action.
__#2 ALPINE GAMBIT   *(C30-019, $1.95)*
__#3 OPERATION COUNTER-SCORCH   *(C30-141, $1.95)*
__#4 TARGET NORWAY   *(C30-121, $1.95)*
__#5 PARTISAN DEMOLITION   *(C30-129, $1.95)*

DIRTY HARRY by Dane Hartman

He's "Dirty Harry" Callahan—tough, unorthodox, no-nonsense plain-clothesman extraordinaire of the San Francisco Police Department inspector #71 assigned to the bruising, thankless homicide detail ...A consummate crimebuster nothing can stop—not even the law! Explosive mysteries involving racketeers, murderers, extortioners, pushers, and skyjackers: savage, bizarre murders, accomplished with such cunning and expertise that the frustrated S.F.P.D. finds itself without a single clue; hair-raising action and violence as Dirty Harry arrives on the scene, armed with nothing but a Smith & Wesson .44 and a bag of dirty tricks; unbearable suspense and hairy chase sequences as Dirty Harry sleuths to unmask the villain and solve the mystery. Dirty Harry—when the chips are down, he's the most low-down cop on the case.